No

Easy

Target

A Wright Series

Book 4

Linda McKown

LINDA MCKOWN

NO EASY TARGET

ISBN-13: 978-0-9997357-3-2

Author:
LindaMcKownAuthor LLC
11574 E Running Deer Trail
Scottsdale, AZ 85262
http://www.lindamckown.com

Any names of people and entities are fictitious in this story having been created by the author's imagination.

Front Cover Photo of the book is copyright through Shutterstock. Book title manipulation was done by Joseph McKown

Dedicated to everyone who has supported me on my journey as a writer. My mother and sister, Marilyn, would have loved this one, because it's about strong, brave women.

Contents

1   Earlier Time with Amy

RANDY MOORE DROVE his motorcycle to a friend's modest house north of San Bernardino, California. Brake Wilson was still in the hospital from an accident, and he was there checking on the goldfish. He wondered about a large man who owned a tiny goldfish named Mackerel. Brake told him to watch out for Raggedy Ann, the golden tabby cat, that roamed his garage and always tried to get in his house.

According to Brake, one day the outdoor cat heard him mention the fish's name. A vision of chunks of fish bait appeared in the feline's greedy eyes or so thought his friend. Randy was told to throw out some pieces of pork skin that Brake purchased at the Mexican market. The whole pig skin was in the garage. He told him the skin should keep the cat a distance from the house if Randy threw it real far into the grass. The mice would run to eat the skin, and the outdoor cat would have a field day with the mice. Randy had to admit that there was strange logic working in Brake's brain. His friend was a little unusual which was all right with Randy. He knew that he could trust Brake with any piece of information or secret. The guy was super loyal. He was the best type of friend to have in this business.

He was surprised to see another motorcycle parked in front of the home. Randy knew who the bike owner was, and displeasure crossed his face. He didn't

1

want to visit with his single cousin today. He was tired of the man's bullshit and lies. Per Brake, his cousin was beginning to get into bad stuff like marijuana and cocaine. Rumors also floated around about car thefts in the area. Rival gang turf fights were also riveting news that surrounded his cousin and the group of males he controlled. Randy wouldn't call them the honorable name of men. He wondered what the next illegal and disastrous business his cousin would try.

"Thugs and thieves. Which force was worst? Every single one of them." He knew all their grimy, groady faces and their motorcycle colors.

Leaving the parked motorcycles, he peeked into the garage and sure enough there was the huge, ugly pig in a large dry cleaner bag with brazen pink lettering, "Rose's Tattoo and Dry-cleaning, High Quality Service". He knew the location of the business, and it wasn't in the best part of town. He would have to let Brake know where another drycleaner store existed. Randy opened the bag and smelled the skin. He shook his head as a swarm of flies tried to get inside.

"I don't think I'm going to eat barbeque pork sandwiches for some time. Besides, shouldn't this thing be in a huge cooler?"

He broke off a piece of skin and the huge body swung, scraping bacon oil on his arm. He tied the bag shut and left the garage. Randy was glad that he was leaving the area to visit his chef friend, Juan, in Mexico. His friend was teaching a three-month cooking class and invited Randy, who wanted to start his own small restaurant business. Juan wanted to join Randy in his new venture by providing some capital and his prized recipes. The two men would develop easy menu items for the startup. Randy was excited and ready to leave as soon as he fed the darn fish and threw the skin out for the Raggedy Ann cat's entertainment.

While staring at the second motorcycle, he heard a step on the patio tile and turned. It was Amy in her long hair, gray leather biker jacket, and burgundy pantsuit with black zippers. It wasn't her outfit that drew his attention, but the black pistol pointed directly at him.

Randy immediately raised his hands in the air dropping the pork belly on the spotted lawn. He wondered what he had done to piss her off or had she found out about his leaving? He believed that his exit would upset her. That was why he hadn't told her. Someone tipped her off. This was exactly the reason why she had the deadly look in her eyes.

"I can explain," said Randy.

She shook her head. "No, you can't."

"Amy, please put the gun away before you hurt someone."

"I want to hurt someone. Don't move!" She raised the pistol higher.

Now, he was alarmed. "Do you want me to get down on my knees and say that I'm sorry? I will if you promise not to shoot."

"No, I'm debating whether I can hit the bee on your arm except it kept moving toward your shirt pocket and back to the same spot. Besides, you smell like old bacon. Ick!"

3

Randy looked at his arm and quickly flicked the bee off. He didn't trust her shot. Right now, the bee was a safer enemy, but it needed to be gone.

"You're a spoil sport." Amy moved the gun lower but didn't put it away. She pouted her lips.

Women, who gave him that look stopped him cold in his tracks. He hated pouted lips which were always close to the next phase called crying-jag. Then he thought about the gun. He remembered that emotions tightened a person's grip. Randy had an ugly thought and was unsure where exactly the barrel was aimed. He chose to wait her out, not wanting to appear under any type of duress. He told himself to stay calm. It was a better way to handle the current emotionally-charged and very sticky situation.

Lately, Amy was like a package wrapped full of dynamite. Everyone knew Skid Peters married her quickly one day in a heat of drunken passion and then divorced her even faster. Evidently, she had loved the diver dude and wasn't ready to end their relationship. Her emotions were on a roller coaster, burning the last high track into a thousand pieces as she traveled down. Fire cracker sparks hit the ground from the racing blast of rubbed metal. The metal, dirt, and rocks popped up more than six feet in the air before turning to ash. The ash-covered roller coaster was also looking like a safer place than Brake's yard.

Randy knew Amy could blow his head off or make love to him. He hoped that it was the latter. His own relationship with a woman had backfired. She left him for another guy, so he had been there. He briefly wondered what his old girlfriend, Sandra, was doing. He told himself to not go down the lane of those memories. Randy thought guys were better at walking away or maybe it was a show of indifference. Men didn't want anyone to know about their failure and played brave warrior. Women, on the other hand, didn't care what people thought, unless it was something about fashion. A woman would create a hen party over lost love just to have other women, who had also been there, help console her.

The two people in the yard were a strange pair of leftover remnants. Both were in rebound mode when they ran into each other. It really wasn't any accident. She followed him to the acreage Randy had purchased for his restaurant. There was an old tool shed on the property, and he made love to her on a decrepit yellow-painted farm table. The minute they had sex, he wished he hadn't. Their sexual activity could cause major problems. She had started dating his crazy cousin, who would kill him deader than a doorknob, if he knew about their affair. His cousin wouldn't even blink when the gun fired, and Randy would be gone in less than a heartbeat with a hole to his head

Amy smiled and threw the gun on the outside plastic chair. She was fortunate that Brake put a straw cushion on his plastic chairs. The gun didn't accidentally click off. She came up to him and unzipped his pants. There was only one more thing she wanted from him before he left. Randy felt obliged to give it to her. What could one more time hurt? They had always been best friends. Sex was a next step. First, he needed to make sure she was alone.

"Why do you have my cousin's bike and, I might add, his very powerful gun? I assume that it's loaded. He doesn't keep guns in the house which are not loaded."

She said flippantly. "Were you a little scared? You do look shaken. That was fun."

Randy wanted to shake her.

"I stole them for a little while. Your cousin drove to Reno, Nevada, to do a deal with some of his new friends. His people don't dare stop me because if they try, I will tell. They've decided to play ignorant and not get involved. I'll refill the gas tank and he won't ever know. He has no clue how many miles are on the bike. He forgets the important stuff. I must always remind him to put air in the tires or to pick up his medicine. Sometimes, he is such a child. The only numbers that he likes have dollar signs attached and lots of commas."

"Still, you're taking an unnecessary risk."

"I don't care. He doesn't tell me what to do."

Randy looked at her. She was close and smelled of flowers. She was important to him and worth the delicious risk. He was feeling confident and good. The vibrations of sweetness were bouncing between them. Or perhaps, it was relief she was no longer mad at him. Without thinking any further, he picked her up and grabbed the cousin's pistol. Carrying her inside the screened porch area, he gently laid her on the beat-up wicker couch with frayed cushions. The gun was carefully placed on a table out of her reach with the safety re-engaged. Her arms came around him in an embrace, leaving no question in Randy's mind where she was focused. He was granted amnesty. He would take it and run with the moment. It was better than holes and threads in his shirt made by bullets. He was ready to be used.

Their clothes hit the wood floor in disarray as their combined body heat and blood pressure rose, competing with the day's temperature. Their high heat won, hands down. Both were satisfied with their private time together. The day was a quiet space in time they both needed. He was glad she followed him and vice versa. Loneliness was held at bay for a while.

The air finally cooled. Randy turned on the small radio and twirled the dial to a music station. They stayed there on the porch until sundown, laughing, and drinking the last of Brake's beer. Finally, they hopped on their bikes and went their separate ways. The engine noises disappeared in the night.

XXXXXX

Halfway out of Los Angeles, Randy remembered the fish. Pulling over to the side of the road, he called another friend of Brake's named Caro. Caro knew where the key was to Brake's home and would feed both critters. She had cans of cat food in her cupboard. Raggedy Ann would get a treat this evening. She told him the cat was a male. Brake had missed those items because the cat was gaining weight lately.

She called the cat Sam. Randy hung up and couldn't stop himself from laughing.

He and Caro had talked a long time about his friend. He got the impression that she liked Brake. Caro was also picking up Brake from the hospital tomorrow. Randy asked her to stop and get the box of donuts that he ordered for his friend and a case of bottled beer. Caro told him she made an enchilada casserole, too. She knew what type of bottled beer. She would bring her own surprise for Brake--a six-pack of peanut-butter beer. The man had large jars of peanut butter in his cupboards along with French bread and grape jelly. She thought he might want to at least try the stuff. It was better than the pepper beer she bought him last Christmas. The pepper beer was from a biker-friend who made the homemade stuff. Brake had complained the Christmas beer was a little on the hot side when he ate the pepper in the empty bottle. Randy was doubtful about the peanut-butter beer. He wouldn't be buying any for his new restaurant unless they came up with a fresher taste nor would he have any pork bellies on his property. However, the pickled squid might work. The Mexican stuff was a little too salty, so he'd have to work on new ingredients. Thanking Caro, he felt better about leaving.

Feeling the wind and smelling the ocean spray, Randy drove on Highway 1 before stopping at a greasy burger joint. He avoided the biker bars but kept his passport and gun handy in his saddlebag. Eating only one of the burgers, he threw the other one in the trash. Randy would learn to make excellent beef enchiladas with sweet red and green sauce. He had been practicing and had a few of his own recipes to share with Juan. Turning onto Highway 5, he would stop in San Diego for the night. He would give his gun to a friend in the morning. His friend owned a pawn shop and would hold it for safekeeping. Then Randy could cross the border.

Memories of Amy drifted across his brain when he hit the motel bed. Quickly, he put her out of his thoughts. Frankly, he didn't have time to worry about her and her relationship with his cousin. He hoped, however, that she would come to her senses. She was a way better person than Minnow Surf. He tried to tell her those facts whenever he could. She just needed to believe them. Little did he know the disastrous trouble Amy would get into before his return from Mexico. Randy would blame Minnow and the forces that ever put them in the same family.

2   Motorcycle Pickup

IT WAS AN almost completely gorgeous day for a motorcycle ride on Highway 215 near San Bernardino, California, when a big rig pulled into Randy Moore's lane. He was almost home and looked upward at the bright blue sky. He was tired from having driven a long way.

"Why me? It was a perfect ride until now."

The traffic was heavy, and he saw an opening in the next lane. Randy Moore stepped on the gas to maneuver around the large cumbersome vehicle. Randy looked in the rearview mirror of his new, priceless motorcycle and saw the police lights flashing. He eased the bike over to the right side of the road and waited. He was glad he left his gun at home this trip. Reaching for his driver's license, registration, and insurance card, Randy heard the eighteen-wheeler trucker honk as he drove by. He saw the truck lights blink, acknowledging there was a Smokey in the area. Randy waved knowing it was too late for him. He knew it was the magic nine miles over the speed limit that caught him. He looked at his speedometer just a few seconds before he saw the police lights. He was over the known-sphere of highway wisdom. All the truckers were wiser than he was on this day and they knew it.

Randy should have stayed at seven miles over the limit or less. Anywhere in the land of the safe zone would have been good. He would be home by now and not have to deal with the law person. The law was usually brisk and efficient. The man he saw looked extremely capable of ruining his day. The officer walked toward Randy and told him he was nine miles per hour over the speed limit.

He got the message loud and clear--Don't go there.

Randy knew he crossed the line and was stupid. "Yes, sir."

"License and registration."

Randy handed them over to the officer.

Several motorcyclists blew by on the freeway honking and blinking their lights which pissed the officer big time. Randy thought everyone in a fifty-mile perimeter would know he was stopped. Then he saw the expression on the officer's face. Things went south from there.

The trucker sent out a message to any known big rig within three hundred miles of the area to proceed with caution due to the Smokey monitoring the highway. The motorcycle boys did the same. All the sports car people were in tune to the CB radio communications at their homes. They received the message, too. There was no fifty-mile perimeter in anyone's world. Those department, compartment of industries slowed down.

It would be many months before this highway saw any ticket land on the desk. The truckers and motorcyclists knew the highway as the dead zone, proceed with high, extremely slow caution. The high-end sports car group found other ways to arrive at their big money paying jobs.

The message was: police occurring at unknown locations and using the highway system in the area as their hunting ground. The watch was initiated due to totally unfriendly-like bears. Another trucker came on the CB-radio and started talking. The bears reminded the trucker of some movie he saw recently. The trucker couldn't recall the name of the show because he was in Brownsville, Texas, gawking at beach babes. All the truckers saw the movie. They recognized the bears. Several truckers on the station grinned because they wanted to go to Brownsville soon. They knew it was the safest place to do a holdover until morning. Also, it was the best place to eat fire-hot tamales wrapped in corn husks. The only soothing drink was tequila with a worm in the bottle. The truckers finished their talk and rolled down the road, passing the amusement park with the bear.

Randy tried to explain to the highway officer that he was maneuvering around the super huge rig spitting heavy rocks which were close to marbles in the racing world. Everyone knew marbles were junk on the track causing the tires to slip. It was a race car driver's nightmare due to the slowdown of friction. Gravity would lift the car and decrease acceleration. He was trying to avoid an accident by accelerating.

The officer frowned and never heard this story before. He called in Randy's license and plate number. Out of the blue, the radio check provided nasty information. The policeman shook his head and immediately arrested Randy which was their new procedure. The wait became longer as a patrol car was called to the scene. A tow truck took the motorcycle into the designated impound lot.

XXXXXX

His lawyer quickly helped remove Randy from the jail cell.

"Randy, why didn't you pay the sixty-five parking tickets that you incurred on the motorcycle in the last three months?"

"I forgot to carry coins for the freaking meters and rolled the tickets into a wad."

The tow truck unloaded Randy's bike in the police building's parking lot next to his lawyer's car. He walked around his motorcycle to make sure there were no scratches or dents. Then he opened his soft leather saddlebag. Taking out a wad of papers rolled together in date order and tied with a black bandana, he held them out to his lawyer.

"Here are the tickets to give to my accountant. Maybe we can deduct them from my business, because most of the tickets are at locations with my clients."

"Great, just what I want to do this afternoon, see your Mr. Flynn."

"Thanks, I really appreciate your legal help today. See you later."

"Oh, Randy, the judge said your driver's license shows expired twenty-one days."

Randy shook his head. "I'll take care of that right away."

He wanted to use foul language but was too mad about the whole mess. He started the motorcycle, enjoying the familiar purr of the engine. Randy smiled after putting on his sunglasses. He buckled the older helmet. It was his favorite to wear on a bright day. There was no music headset in the helmet and he could enjoy the rhythm of the beastly machine. He started to feel better. It was rather worth the ticket, but maybe not the jail cell. While in jail he did invite some of the other boys on each side of him to visit one of his restaurants for a free lunch, courtesy of the owner. He gave them free dinner coupons he carried in his back pocket. The police hadn't removed those paper items.

Randy drove to his restaurant office and went to the smooth wood bar. Changing his mind, he grabbed an orange juice instead. Next, he drove home to his two and a half million-dollar home in the hills of Los Angeles. He wanted to talk to his wife, Sandra. Arriving home, he found her note stating that she went to her beauty shop to change her hairdo. She never liked her hairdo. Her hair always looked fine to him.

Instead, Randy worked on the equipment in his gym for two hours. After taking a shower and putting on his business suit, he knew the gang must be made aware of the new rules and police. He knew the scrutiny of bikers was very much something to do with his cousin, Minnow Surf, and his wife, Amy, who were being released soon. They had been in prison quite some time. It was enough time for him to build his empire. It felt wonderful to be on top of his business game. He worried how his money would sit with Minnow. Getting in his new, sleek sports car, he talked to himself.

"Probably not well at all."

In the meantime, his people would need to be ready for everything that would land upon their territory and them. Picking up his cell phone, he contacted his right-hand man, Brake.

"Tell the gang to drive clean. Oh, they also need to pay all tickets as soon as possible, like today. Maintain correct speed at all times."

"I'm on it."

Drive clean meant the police were searching all motorcycles, vehicles, and them for everything. His gang would remove the illegal wheels, handlebars, engines, mufflers, and swapped license plates. They would need to dump the marijuana, the unopened beer cans, and any other Mexican drug paraphernalia. Weapon removal would be huge as the guns and bullets would need to be removed if they couldn't find their carry permits. If they had their permits, the guns must be locked up. The long knives would be replaced in their leg harnesses with the correct, legal size. All broken lights would be replaced.

Brake called Randy back. "What about my bicycle chain?"

"Total, Brake."

"No sparklers either?" whined Brake.

"None. The gang needs to appear normal."

15

He could hear his man sigh. Randy didn't get the man's passion for fire and camouflage. His strength in tossing a bicycle chain the furthest at their beer parties was a symbol of pride. There was nothing normal about any member of the gang.

Brake took the ten bottles of beer out of his soft saddlebag. He couldn't remember how old the beer was until he tasted one. The full bottles went into the garbage. Brake would buy the more expensive beer next time. They lasted longer.

The bicycle chain went into Brake's bedroom draped over his mirror like it was a large first place rosette from an international cat show. He did, however, leave his small opener, cigarettes, and lighter in the right saddlebag. He left his green camouflage vest in a roll in the left one. Trying to think up new equipment that was police-safe kept him busy for two days.

Randy drove back to his restaurant in his expensive black sports car, having parked his motorcycle in the garage. He wanted the police to see him as a polished, rich businessman, not a gang member. He knew Sandra already wore the image having seen the price tags on her dresses and shoes. His wife kept an entire room in the house for those two items. He was granted two small closets in the house.

Randy wondered how long it would take the Los Angeles investigator, Derek Wright, to arrive on his door step. He went out to talk to his security people about Minnow and Derek. One of the men was dangerous. The bad guys always made up their own rules and were the first to start a brawl. It usually was in a bar, nightclub, or restaurant, and he owned quite a few of those types of businesses. Randy felt uneasy about the future. The Wright man would be easier to handle.

3 Background

IT ALL STARTED with Derek and Jess Wright moving their eighty-five-foot motorboat from Los Angeles to San Diego where War Julio Samba waited to purchase their wonderful, fully loaded ship. It was just not any ship with helicopter, but it was Dean Crain's. Dean was the original owner who gave the motorboat to the Wrights after he died. The boat contained hidden guns, special secret closets, and gear. It was a dream of a boat, an off-the-charts ship, with special stereo sound and all the latest technological wonders onboard. It even had its own separate tank to put out fire. Computers and cameras were everywhere.

Derek and Jess were buying a super yacht with a larger helicopter to accommodate their family and growing circle of crony friends. Their boat would also be fully loaded with guns and the latest technological gear. Having sold their home, they were taking the older boat to San Diego to pick up their newly purchased, converted 2009 yacht which was approximately one-hundred-sixty-feet long. Then they would cruise both ships to Curacao where Jess and Derek would live with their children. Curacao was the location of War Julio's fishing business.

Derek would work with the police and the Miami cronies on the plan to stop and catch Amy and

Minnow Surf. Their release from prison was a huge problem because both threatened to kill the Wright's children after they were released. That was why the Wrights were moving their children to Curacao.

Jess felt the presence of evil in the area and didn't tell Derek that she thought she was Minnow's target. Her elderly friend, Louisa Renaliere, warned her in the past. Louisa saw a picture of Minnow being moved from one holding cell to his final prison. He smiled and showed the photographer a torn photo in his hand which contained only a picture of Jess. Louisa knew about the Wright family from a newer friend, Dean Crain, who visited her before he died. She checked out the Wrights. Her computer store clerk installed photo software for Louisa and showed her how to use the program. She found a person must blow up the picture on the computer to see the photograph better. Louisa contacted the newspaper and found out the name of the photographer. She contacted him and found out the words written on the back of the photograph that was in Minnow's hand.

The Wrights and the local police were upset about the early release of the Surfs. They believed they also had been involved in a couple of homicides earlier. The police found two dead gang member's bodies that correlated to the time before Minnow went to jail. This raised more suspicion around Minnow Surf. Skid Peters, who used to be married briefly to Amy, was questioned. Photos of the two dead men were shown to him from prior police files. He told Derek the dead men were two separate gang leaders involved in illegal drugs and robberies. He had seen them talking with Minnow on several occasions. They were competitors of Minnow Surf. The police figured Minnow took over their operations. They began heavily monitoring the gang.

Derek was hired by the police to investigate the murders while remaining undercover. Derek contacted his friend, Jim Michaels, for help. He would fly back to Los Angeles when things heated up.

4   Amy and Minnow Surf

AMY AND MINNOW Surf were to be released from prison through a special deal. They were allowed out of their sentence by five years for information they provided to the police. The two people were married but hadn't seen each other for ten years. Their first meeting would be formal and casual. They would live together in a five-hundred-thousand-dollar house purchased for them by Minnow's cousin, Randy Moore.

Then the distance between Amy and Minnow would grow. The breakage of family would occur. Storm clouds would develop due to the unstable air. The super cell storm would produce the funnel. The funnel would appear approaching tornado wind speeds. It wasn't one funnel, but two, on a high-speed collision course, spinning counterclockwise out of control. The older con artists knew when to leave the area. They were headed toward safer earthquake zones.

The newbies would be caught in the fray. If the two tornados collided, it could be the big bomb blast all over again. The scales would level and pull the two funnels apart. The wind speeds, however, would reach somewhere in the hundred miles per hour range. They would move beyond the normal one-hundred-twelve mile per hour range.

The destruction would be sporadic and rampant in certain parts of California. In some areas, level F-3 winds would approach one hundred fifty-eight to a little over two hundred miles per hour. A race car could travel within the range and possibly a little faster on a winning speedway track. People would wish they were in a race car so they, too, could leave the area and win the right to live.

The separation of Minnow and Amy Surf, of course, would be the perfect break the police required to infiltrate the illegal games of the Green Stream gang who were the real evil ones. There were other gangs, but they weren't near as bad.

"What makes a person fall prone to evil? Is it the right circumstance or is our environment to blame? Isn't crazy exactly what it is? Mentally unsound comes to mind."

In Minnow's case, it was parents who never worked, but used all the agencies at their disposal to get free housing, free food, and free help. They worked harder to get out of work than anyone he knew. All types of ailments and diseases would befall them after they visited the local clinic. The clinic was their shopping mall to pick up information. With the information they could correctly act out their symptoms. The bathroom counter was a druggie's delight with every kind of pharmacy-labeled bottle available.

The parents taught Minnow how to steal one Christmas morning, showing him where he could borrow two new, ten-speed bicycles left on someone's front lawn. They put heavy emphasis on the word: loaner. The parents waited down the street in a beater truck while Minnow and his sister, Annabelle, confiscated the loaners. Then Minnow stole black spray paint and special mirrors. He ripped off the fender guard on the back of the bike and sold it. The bikes were totally disguised with the bicycle tabs removed and serial numbers filed off. He also stole cigarette papers and tobacco from the store to roll his own cigarettes. He told himself that the cigarettes were more loaners. Minnow didn't do the e-cigarettes. They were more difficult to hide and weren't ergonomically-friendly. He was trying to save the earth and keep things green. "No use polluting the water."

The loaner experience was major and later led to the chop-shop owned by Minnow of stolen sports cars. Smoking cigarettes led to smoking marijuana. Everything didn't stop there, he required more in the way of illegal activities. The stealing and lying increased so much so that the original innocent child was lost. The con artist arrived, shoving goodness from every corner of his life. A new, more heinous persona would appear. Narcissism at its finest joined in.

Amy's parents were no better. They drove around in their beater car until they saw a brand-new car. They flipped a Kennedy coin to see which person was going to play patsy. They would pull in front of the new car, slam on their brakes, and cause an accident. Then they sued the other party for whiplash. Either her father or mother were in a neck brace constantly. When Amy told them that their activity was not right, they told her she could leave. They didn't intend to be poor. Her parents told Amy that she would never amount to anything because she was weak. She would be the poor one. That made Amy mad. She went to the drugstore and got a job as a sales clerk. She worked there during high school. That's where she met Minnow who was at the pharmacy counter. He seemed like a friendly guy. He was picking up his allergy medicine. He told her that he was allergic to peanuts. She felt sorry for him.

After her divorce, Amy hooked up with Minnow because he seemed to have a never-ending flow of money which he spent on her. He told her that she didn't need to work. Because he loved her, he would take care of her. She hated hand-me-down clothes, and Minnow bought brand new ones. They weren't designer clothes, but they smelled new. Amy anticipated the money flow happening close to Minnow was a place she wanted to exist. Then she could leave and never come back to her parent's dysfunctional home. At the time, it didn't matter where the money came from. At least he didn't wear a neck brace and steal from young families. He only stole from the rich. Amy moved in with Minnow. She would get indoctrinated to the ways of the gang called Green Stream.

Amy also liked Minnow's cousin, Randy Moore, and one night made love to him. Randy was good looking, tall, and strong. Amy didn't dare tell Minnow because the flow of money to her would stop, and he would kill Randy. She snuck off and saw Randy one more time because they were more than friends. He always treated her nice. She would later wonder if she made a mistake and married the wrong man. Every woman sometimes had that thought. Amy dismissed her misgivings about Minnow.

5   Randy Moore and Trouble

RANDY STRETCHED AND felt confident. He finally made it in this world. He hated the newer Green Stream gang and worked hard to rid himself of his past and Minnow Surf. He owned five legal, profitable restaurants, and just opened a dance nightclub. He owned several other holdings and obtained a good accountant and lawyer. Randy was smart and cautious.

He retained the good guys from the old gang whom he called his motorcycle friends. They helped Randy whenever he needed it. Randy was busy and let his motorcycle comrade, Brake, lead the motorcycle gang. It would be good experience and teach him leadership. The gang gave Brake his nickname because his brakes failed one time on a dirt road. Brake landed in one of those rolled haystacks, having traveled a good forty feet in the air, barely clearing the barbed wire fence with his two-hundred-seventy-five-pound frame.

Following Brake's motorcycle, Randy helped him by calling for an ambulance, police, and their gang to pick up the damaged motorcycle. All the gang chipped in to repair the bike with Randy contributing significantly. Brake never forgot that incident. Randy was his friend for life.

Purchasing the nightclub, Randy didn't have to hold parties in his two-and-a-half-million-dollar house anymore. The Minnow-controlled thugs would have to buy their own food, drinks, and pay to get into his nightclub. It was another layer of security to keep them out.

He dreaded the idea that Minnow was out of jail. He saw nothing but trouble on the horizon. Randy knew Minnow's chop-shop rented the sports car to a London woman who tried to kill an investigator called Derek Wright. Only the attempt was on Derek's wife who was driving her husband's car.

That little episode made Randy want to move to Mexico. He could be listed as an accessory by the police and it would take his lawyer a year to get him out of jail from the clogged mess of delay by the court system. He couldn't afford to do anything illegal.

Randy noted the recently-found dead gang member's bodies were Minnow's competitors and he figured Minnow killed them. Randy was furious with Minnow but had no evidence to show his group.

Then there was the problem of Amy. Randy wasn't sure how he felt about her, but things were not going too well lately with his wife, Sandra. All she wanted to do was get beauty creams, attend expensive spas, and plump something on her body up or down. She complained constantly about her looks and wanted to see a plastic surgeon.

Randy put his foot down and told her that she was beautiful enough and he wouldn't pay for any procedure, so now she was mad at him. He knew somehow, he said the words wrong to his wife. Randy meant he loved her anyway. That only upset Sandra more.

He knew not to mention the hormone word. Randy believed there should be an online manual on how to talk to a woman and not get in trouble. It would read, "If all else fails, jump into the ocean, and drift towards the safer shore."

Needing to hire some more bartenders for his nightclub, Randy looked at several applications. He liked this one applicant and asked his secretary to set up an appointment with some woman who moved to Los Angeles from Miami.

Randy stepped into his black sports car, because he must keep a meeting with Minnow at one of Randy's restaurants and wondered, "What in the heck does the guy want now. The house and two new vehicles should be payment enough from me to satisfy family matters."

Randy met Minnow.

"I want to open a store to sell guns, but can't because of my criminal record, so I need you to open the shop under your name."

Randy slowly looked at Minnow. If a person ran into a series of bad days or bad people, he was screwed in spades. Randy thought he should just give up and become a cynical person. He wanted to move on quickly to Mexico or take a cruise his wife was pressuring him to enjoy. Right now, the cruise was looking like a great escape.

"How many days have passed since you were released from prison?"

"It's about a week now."

"Then it ought to dawn on a person's brain that one must lie low for a while or else the person can quickly find oneself in the familiar confines of concrete and barbed wire. Unless, of course, you want to go back for the soft bed, appetizing food, and play endless card games. Maybe you miss the puzzles."

"No, the food is terrible. The bed and rough sheets are inconceivably bad. I hate the sunshine and develop a sunburn in the exercise yard. It is a torture yard and I'm not going back. Well, that's why I absolutely need your help. I'm here talking to you for an important reason and you know I hate puzzles. The pieces never fit together correct and someone usually stole a few pieces. The whole picture is ruined."

Randy stood over Minnow. Minnow was forced to look up to the man in power. "The answer is no way in my lifetime. You can make do with your existing businesses. By the way, your current business projects don't meet parole-qualified minimum requirements either. Besides, I have paid you back in spades with the nice home and two vehicles. I'm through with helping you and anything illegal. Are you clear?"

"It isn't enough. I was in prison a long time, away from my important businesses. It will take me time to ramp up the current ones. I must get more money right away. You should help me because you have so much money which you keep too close. I would print money, but I don't own plates or a have access to a good printer. My printer is too old. I can't even buy the color thing and there's not much ink in my black one."

Randy glared at Minnow. He was amazed at how the man's brain skewed things into unreality.

"I'll send over a new printer, but you are still so lost."

Randy left his restaurant with a pissed off Minnow fuming in his chair.

His cousin, Randy, always made him feel inferior. Minnow couldn't kill Randy because he might need him in the future or the use of his restaurant and nightclub for his meetings. Besides Randy was respected by his people. That could present problems he didn't want to tangle with now. Randy was stronger.

Minnow called his gang and told them to bring outrageous amounts of beer because he wanted to have a party. He told them to bring women and pizza, too. It was one of those times when Minnow made a bad decision and found it was an unforgiveable and uncorrectable one. The number of bad decisions would increase. Randy was correct. Minnow's alibis wouldn't work in the future. He would be lost shortly, a loner and a loser.

6   After Effects

THE PROBLEM WITH the party was that no one told Amy. She went shopping and graced the beauty shop specifically for a trim and highlight of gorgeous color. She picked a beautiful leopard print dress at a specialty shop and bought sexy black strappy heels. It was a fun day for her.

Amy forgot how wonderful and free the female shopping experience was for a woman. The beauty products and new lipstick colors were in a pretty bag she dropped on the seat of her new car. She patted her new bag and was pleased Randy sent her a check special-delivery, so she could have a fun day. She didn't give the check to Minnow or tell him about it. She wanted her new look to be a surprise. She wanted him to see the new impressive woman, not some haggard jailbird. Amy missed that womanly experience called Rodeo Drive.

She had her nails and toenails done in clear polish with gold dust, and a touch of black. For the first time in a long time, she felt new and in her element. The paint wash of jail was gone. Amy looked fine. Confidence factor rolled into her world.

Next, she drove to Randy's new nightclub to check it out and thank him properly. She drove by his

31

nice house earlier in the morning and saw him leave. Amy wanted to talk with Randy alone without the wife.

His black powerful and stable sports car was in the back of the nightclub in his private parking space. She pulled into the next space because it was also marked private. Amy was ushered into Randy's nice plush office.

Randy moved from his desk and came over to Amy. He held her in his arms, then forced himself to move away from her. She looked good, exotic, and smelled too good. Memories hit him in his lower extremities.

Amy smiled. She knew the look of a man with desirous feelings.

"Would you like some refreshment? I can get you coffee or anything stronger?"

"Hello, Randy."

She really looked at the handsome man in his nice shirt with rolled-up sleeves. She saw his lightweight navy sports coat near a chair.

"Why didn't you come to visit me?"

Randy swallowed. He remembered the time she held the pistol in her hands.

"I thought it best to give you some time to get yourself looking exceptionally beautiful. You did capture the exotic look."

"Yes, I now look beautiful, but not good enough to kiss?"

It was Randy's turn to smile and said, "When a woman wants, she wants. I can see that I forgot that is your favorite expression."

Randy came over to Amy and kissed her long and held her. Then he walked over to the window looking out in distress.

"I value my life and yours too much to repeat kissing you again. Plus, I do love my wife."

"Yes, I remember catching you during a down time in your life when Sandra did marry someone else."

She knew he loved Sandra a long time. It was lucky for him that Sandra divorced the other man. Then there were her years wasting away in a jail with all doors locked.

"This kiss between us will always be about good friends. I value both our lives, but I came to ask you an additional favor," pleaded Amy.

"What can I assist you with this time? You are welcome to ask me. I will be here for you as a good friend."

Amy felt relieved. She had really counted on his help. She didn't want to be poor but being around her husband wasn't working too well. She could tell after a week with him. There was a difference and the toll of years formed a deep wedge in her thinking. She no longer was an innocent.

"I might need a job. If I had my own money, I could leave Minnow. My husband scares me with maniacal talk about killing children. He also did refinance our home to have money to buy a gun business."

Randy looked at Amy in alarm.

"Crap, crap, crap! I hadn't even thought of that event. What a sneaky jerk? Besides, half the house is yours as a gift."

"Yes, I know. I did sign the refinance papers and probably shouldn't have done so. Not a smart move at all. I wanted the money to stop the craziness. I'm wrong to think it will stop. My husband still is set on killing Derek Wright's family as revenge for being sent to prison."

"I thought those comments were just talk to scare people. What is with the man's insane ideas and suicidal need to buy a gun business?"

"Minnow is plotting."

Amy looked at Randy.

"The plotting is wrong. My husband will harm me and drag me into the heat. My life is now valuable. I can't go back to jail again. I won't help him anymore."

"Is Minnow plain stupid?"

"Yes, purely a stupid person. Because the Wright family has left the country and are nowhere to be found. I do listen to my husband's conversations."

Randy knew revenge could ruin a man.

"I'm glad the Wrights left and will be safe. They are rich and can live anywhere they want."

Randy looked at Amy's eyes, and they both felt the same trap door descending due to Minnow.

"I will help you anyway I can. There is a job available as extra hostess anytime you need one. I also own several apartment buildings if you need a place to live. I already plan to upgrade security at one of the buildings."

"Great, I'll let you know." She rose to leave the room. "And, thanks."

He walked her out to her car and smiled again. "Everything will be all right."

"Don't try to con me. This is bullshit. Things always turn worse around Minnow."

Randy made an appointment to meet with his lawyer. He didn't want to become the fall guy to some con artist game created by Minnow Surf. He could feel the creepy target setup game happening every minute he talked with the little mastermind. Randy was preparing his house for war. He also paid a photographer to secretly take pictures of Minnow at his various illegal businesses.

Amy drove to a restaurant and ate supper because Minnow didn't answer his phone. She texted him approximately when she would arrive home. There was no reply from him. Eventually, she arrived home late at nine-thirty to see several cars leave. Amy walked into the kitchen to see empty beer bottles everywhere and twenty-five pizza boxes almost empty.

The living room was the same way, a total absolute mess. There were ashtrays sitting on the floor. The house smelled of rot-gut beer. Tiny torn fabric showed in the armrest of the new couch which was growing into larger holes by the minute. The cushion contained greasy cheese spots. Orange cheese doesn't wash out. The grease would only grow larger. The carpet was smeared with some red tomato sauce near the two designer chairs.

The damaged house reminded her of her parent's home. It was a space she couldn't live. Her husband knew those pieces of information. Yet, he brought this madness into her living room.

"Correction, he brought hell into my half of the house."

She would have to hire cleaners tomorrow or she could leave. Maybe it was time to let him clean his own mess. Things hadn't changed with her husband. He was doing the same tricks. Amy remembered prior jail years and apartments that looked just like her new screwed-up house. Plus, there was more than the house that got screwed as she would quickly find out.

Amy walked into the bedroom and there was her drunk, passed out husband in his underwear. The bed was unmade. She made the new bed with the pretty exotic bedspread before she left that day. Sandra helped decorate their home, remembering Amy's likes and dislikes. The exotic bedspread and her life were now in the toilet. She saw some lipstick on her bedspread. It was not one of the colors she wore.

Their home was once clean and beautiful. It was a kind gesture from Randy to include her name on the house title. Amy felt the silver tarnish wearing off the cheap wedding ring from Minnow. Her life with him was cheap. The tarnish dissolved into a puddle of tears on their bedroom carpet. The only thing she saw was the dead lead color obscuring her world.

Amy was not stupid, but her husband had amazingly accelerated to the top of the list. It was as if she suddenly awakened from a bad fever. The reality of her life and downfall due to her marriage to Minnow was brought forefront. She wiped away the last of her tears. Amy felt like running from the scene. She didn't want to play the game with her husband of hurt wife, apologize, and repeat it the next day. It was a tilted, bent merry-go-round and she was getting off.

"This story ends now. You're lucky that I don't have your old pistol. I could kill you today and not feel a thing."

She went outside to remove herself for a few minutes from hate and emptiness. The fresh air brought back sweet memories with someone else, her best friend. Clearing her throat, she called Randy.

"I'll take your job as hostess. When can I start? Oh, I do need an apartment, too. Maybe the building with the upgraded security. Can I get a short-term loan from my first paycheck? And do you know a good lawyer?"

Randy would get things rolling for her. There would be no loan. He would give her an immediate bonus.

The winds were picking up speed because damage was done. She felt betrayed. Amy knew her husband's crimes. She kept their prison letters. She went to the bedroom and packed her clothes, shoes, makeup, and letters with secret writings on the stamps. Outside the door stood a tan box with large lettering, PRINTER. She threw the box in the trunk of her car. There was no use leaving a new printer for Minnow to break. Amy would later open a bank lockbox and place the prison letters inside along with another letter. Amy knew the harm her husband could do.

She wondered if she should carry a gun. It would be illegal for her to do so per her parole officer because of her prison record. Amy didn't buy an illegal gun, but Minnow did. He didn't care about laws.

Amy started caring and kept all her parole officer appointments. She would change her life.

7   Rhonda as Bartender

RHONDA WHITE ADJUSTED her parachute one last time. The plane signaled her it was time for the jump. She signaled back and exited the airplane. Counting to herself, she pulled the ripcord. The parachute deployed.   Loving, the lighter weight parachutes, she saw the road and her landmark building and parking lot. She touched ground about three-quarters a mile from the building which was where she intended to land.

Checking her large wristwatch, the time was correct. The owner of the building should be approaching shortly. She stuffed the lightweight chute into the pack, unhooking everything. A black sports car pulled up.

"Are you lost? This is a private road. I can help you if you need directions. Is that a parachute?"

Rhonda laughed. This guy was rather cute, but very married.

"I know exactly where I have landed."

She pointed to her watch, "Guidance system big time."

Randy frowned.

Rhonda felt exhilarated. She loved the rush of jumping. Her eyes and face showed her delight.

"I have to attend a meeting with the owner of this fancy nightclub down the road. I thought I would add a little pleasure today before the joint discussion started."

Randy really looked at the beautiful, very independent, stunning woman.

"You aren't by any chance the applicant named Rhonda White from Miami who applied for a bartender position?"

"Yes, I'm the woman and you most definitely must be the owner or someone equally important to be driving an amazing vehicle which is a super powerful machine, not to mention very shiny and clean."

Randy stepped out of the car and introduced himself. Rhonda stored her gear in his trunk and sunk down in plush leather seats.

She knew the interview would go well. Randy shook his head at the woman's unbelievable entrance for a job. Rhonda told him it was her favorite hobby and jumping kept her at top performance. The sky was her gym.

Randy smiled and needed this nightclub to be upscale. The woman was exactly what was required.

"This is an interesting day. Let's go to the restaurant and do the interview. I'm sure we can work together."

Rhonda could hardly wait to tell Tami Cortez about her landing and interview. She was proud of the fact that she was good at her game. Stealth mode was her specialty. Tami was her contact person to relay information back to Derek Wright, the Los Angeles investigator working with the police. Rhonda knew it was a perfectly good day, because she was hired.

She took the tour of the nightclub and was introduced to the security team. Rhonda gave a few suggestions to Randy regarding his on-tap keg beer selections and the arrangement of the liquor at the bar. She knew how everything should lay out for selection and enticement for the customers.

Randy hired Rhonda to do the same arrangement with his other restaurant bar areas.

Randy was pleased with his new employee. He trusted her worldly expertise. His beer business and liquor business profits increased. She convinced Randy to let his chefs try fish from War Julio Samba's fishing empire in Curacao. War Julio was a good friend of hers. She told him the fish was to-die-for.

After tasting the fish, Randy gave his chefs authority to create a new vendor profile and change their menu. Rhonda's comment about the fish were correct. People flocked to his restaurants for the seafood of the day. Rhonda was the piece of gold expertise that he'd been looking for to move his restaurants up a notch.

8   Jess and Derek's Yacht

THEIR   ONE-HUNDRED-SIXTY-FOOT, *Silver Zephyr,* a custom, redesigned, white 2009 super yacht, was a grand thing to see arrive at their new dock space in San Diego harbor.

Jess excitedly turned to Derek who quickly grabbed his beautiful blonde wife in her red jumpsuit and high heels to give her a kiss and hug. Her hair was up in a loose chignon with a gold barrette. Derek laughed because he loved taking barrettes out of her long hair.

Her gray mist eyes sparkled with pleasure. Derek was immensely pleased he purchased the used larger yacht. The red helicopter was repainted to include on the side a large series of varying width gray bands that faded into a white ocean wave.

Everything was about Jess, but this purchase was for their family as well. The twenty-million-dollar yacht was worth it. The money from an earlier sunken ship treasure find off the coast of Dakar, Senegal, Africa, Jess's book revenues, and her clothing plus perfume line helped pay toward the purchase price of the yacht.   Their deceased friend, Dean Crain's warehouse holdings paid them handsomely each year for additional revenue.

She loved the navy jacket, white shirt, and gray slacks she bought him. Her brown haired, six-foot, many-muscled husband looked great. He turned his brown eyes toward her. He was glad they had this private moment with each other.

They decided they wanted to toast champagne to their deceased friend, Dean Crain, alone and tour the boat. The others would arrive three hours later. Derek arranged a quick vegetarian lunch together with the help of their chef. There would be many hot and cold hors d'oeuvres, cake, and champagne later for the christening of the ship with their children and friends.

They sat down at one of the tables. Derek opened the champagne and poured in special champagne glasses etched with SZ and a wave swirl. The entire glass selection and dinnerware were designed after the name of their ship and any waters she might encounter.

"To Dean. We honor you for your love and guidance."

"A salute to Dean. Thank you."

They toasted, and Derek took the remote for the state-of-the-art stereo sound system and hit number six which was her favorite calypso song. It also was the signal to the chef to bring out their gourmet lunch salads of lobster and crab with two side dressings of strawberry and lemon. Jess loved it. Then they toured their yacht.

The yacht was built to accommodate ten to twelve guests and eight crew members. The yacht's cruise speed was fourteen knots with top speed at seventeen knots via twin diesel engines for a combined total of thirty-six hundred horsepower. Derek would have liked a little more speed but thought they could work on that issue next year.

There was a total of five staterooms on the yacht. Each stateroom had its own shower and bath. The guest staterooms were on the interior deck below their master and small living space. The crew and galley kitchen area were also on the interior deck. The kitchen included top-end professional equipment to accommodate their parties.

Jess stepped into the master stateroom through sliding glass doors from the main deck. She chose navy and silver as the color theme throughout the yacht with a hint of coral-red thrown in the mix. The cabinetry throughout the yacht was satin mahogany with gray marble tops. She was amazed at the remote-control silver shades. Their carpet was a darker gray. The quilt was a custom navy comforter with their SZ wave logo imprinted in silver. Jess created the larger sophisticated design. The views from the master bedroom windows were one-hundred-eighty-degrees.

The glass was special designed bullet-proof and difficult to see inside the stateroom from outside. The bath contained a marble shower with two sprayers and mood lighting. She was amazed how large the closets were and there were also hidden closets. There was a marble-topped computer desk with two comfortable desk chairs. Their living area contained a silver-colored, soft leather couch and ottoman with a flip tray top. The especially exquisite, ultra-modern, silver crystal light had been installed. The light made Jess smile.

Derek grabbed her and kissed her long and slow.

"We need to wait until later."

"I hate that word unless I say it to you when you're trying on sexy lingerie."

Derek sighed, he would have to wait.

They were staying on the yacht together without children that evening. Jim and Mary Beth Michaels were staying with their children at the Michaels' home as was Skid Peters and his daughter, Maggie.

"I love the coral color roses you brought me."

She squeezed his arm. "I want to see the rest of our yacht. It is hard not to call it a motorboat or ship."

"Yes, I'm struggling with the new words. I will show you all the hidden closets, nets, and weaponry gear later. I forgot to tell you that our captain and mates think the yacht is the absolute best thing they ever crewed. The captain is busy reading the manuals on all the systems, thrusters, generators, electronics and emergency procedures to get up-to-date. The chef is assessing our supplies we'll require for our trip."

"I believe our yacht is the best, too. It is more, more, more."

"Honey, if you say more once again, our guests must wait another hour to come onboard. You know how to drive me crazy."

She reached up and kissed her sweet husband softly. Derek picked her up and twirled her around and put her down. It was going to be a good night.

The main deck showed a bar and dining area with a table that folded away completely or could be made large enough to accommodate twelve guests. They chose comfortable chairs rather than a large lounge sofa. That way, the chairs could be maneuvered into different configurations or removed below if needed.

The step-up to the outside main deck contained a spa where the cover could be opened or closed. Once closed, the floor could be used for dancing. The padded lounge chairs retracted into the sides of the yacht when not in use as did the side tables. There was a large barbeque and mini bar near the other inside bar.

The upper deck contained a small area reserved for the helicopter called the heli-pad, indoor exercise room, bathroom, small shower, and elevator to four levels. There were stairs to the pilothouse or bridge area and back down to the kitchen and crew quarters. The glass on the bridge was also bulletproof and sun-glare resistant. The yacht contained satellite and internet communication with plasma televisions throughout.

There was a thirty-foot tender on board for traveling to ports while at anchor plus two ski watercrafts, room for the submarine and small lift crane, and any diving gear. Portable inflatable watercraft with small motors were also stored for quick release and retrieval. All the safety gear possible was on board.

At the last minute, they included an inflatable dock designed to hold the watercraft while at anchor. Special gear was included so they could rig a safety net and zip line between their boat and War Julio's motorboat.

Their special order lifelike robots from the space company would be brought on board the next day and placed in the hold with the freezers. They would use them at their next annual party in Curacao. The boat also contained trash compactors in a separate room.

Their tour was over when the ship's captain announced over the intercom that their guests were arriving. Jess and Derek could hear their happy children. They were glad the large beam yacht with over twenty-nine-and-a-half-feet would accommodate their friends.

Jim was bringing his new camera gear to take pictures of their extravagant tub and their sweet smiling faces.

9   Gang Mentality and Trouble

A GANG WAS really a group of con artists who met and aligned their forces together. The lack of consequences for their actions brought the reward of invisibility to a gang member. Money was also a draw. The truly bad con artist wanted to stay there. Typically, the gang leader elected was the person everyone either liked or feared.

In the Green Stream gang, there were two groups, those that liked Randy Moore as leader and those that followed Minnow Surf as a feared leader. In Minnow's case, perhaps they saw the madness where the reasoning and logic went haywire. There were perception errors which interrupted all normal reactions to the world. Obsession went from mildly anxious to confusion to devil-personified. Control of the mind would slip.

Minnow would merge his people into one large gang machine, overtaking the smaller ones. He was building an empire and people died if necessary. A gun shop owner disappeared when his store was robbed of all weaponry and bullets. The entire shop contents were missing, and the building accidentally burned to the ground.

Blaming Randy for the loss of Amy Surf started the winds of trouble. If Randy hadn't given his wife a job, she wouldn't have left him. Then he found out Randy set her up in an apartment. Next thing he knew,

Randy was buying a beauty shop for his wife, which increased the suppressed anger from Minnow.

Minnow never cleaned the mess in the house. Some of the other gang women threw the garbage into trash bags on occasion due to the smell.

Minnow, in his greed for more money, hooked up with a leader called Matin Domingo, a major player in arms trafficking of illegal weapons and ammunition. Minnow believed if he made more money, Amy would come back to him. There was money waiting for him. It was almost free for the taking. Minnow believed this was his time for a comeback to glory.

Domingo ran the arms from Africa to Curacao with a last destination in Los Angeles. Living in Miami, Domingo heard about the burned gun shop and hired his boys to locate the people responsible. The gun shop was one he used to find the straw buyers. He wanted to find the person who interfered.

Sitting in his huge mansion in a heavily guard-gated, rich community in Florida, Domingo believed the gang thug, Minnow Surf, owed him a favor. Domingo wanted to meet this criminal. He asked his bodyguards to make the arrangements for the trip on his private jet to Los Angeles.

If errors in judgment were a ticket to the lottery, then Minnow would be the winner due to the exorbitant amount of tickets acquired. He made a second blunder and sold some of the stolen guns to a person who sold them to some local terrorists hiding in Oregon. Those stolen guns would be used and land in the hands of the Oregon police who would trace back their serial numbers to the missing gun store owner in Los Angeles, California.

Randy represented the opposite in a gang leader. He was a fully-charged, super ego person and believed in his own worth that pushed him to succeed in the normal world. He was not a prisoner of madness like his cousin. There was no confusion in his every step as he expanded his businesses with his entrepreneurial skills.

Randy was smart and knew to stay away from Amy. He avoided Minnow. He also thought he hadn't ever needed the gang. But he did choose his friends carefully.

He did start sky diving lessons and went with Rhonda after work for training sessions. Rhonda was the instructor at this small sky diving business and she taught him everything she knew. Most specifically, she taught him safety, and he must always check his own pack thirty minutes before a jump, and then to never let it out of his sight or hands.

Even though there was a second safety chute, she was always careful. The AAD or automatic activation device would open the reserve chute at a pre-determined altitude which was part of the required dual parachute system. The reserve shoot was repacked every one-hundred-twenty-days by an FAA certified rigger.

Rhonda told Randy she was certified if he needed help with any equipment. Randy got the message about *trust no one* on your first parachute and trust a valued friend on the second one. It was something he did all his life, trust only close friends.

Randy heard about the police inspecting the burned-out gun shop in the area on the local news channel and again wondered how quickly he could move his restaurants and nightclub to Mexico. He knew it was a small matter of time before all the United States agencies would become involved in this one.

He thought Minnow just entered a more corrupt world and everything would be brought down. Randy put two of his lesser restaurants that were close to Minnow's house up for sale. He didn't want Minnow to use them anymore for his business deals. That would further piss off Minnow.

10   Leaving San Diego

IT WAS TWO weeks since Jess and Derek stepped aboard their yacht in San Diego. Their captain and crew took the ship out to check all the systems and become familiar with them that first week.

While all items were loaded on their ship, the second week, their captain went with War Julio Samba on their newly acquired eighty-five-foot boat to familiarize their captain and crew with all systems.

Finally, everyone was ready to leave San Diego to cruise to their destination in Puerto Vallarta. Skid Peters and Maggie were onboard as were their children, Sami and Justin. It was a balmy ninety degrees as the smaller boat headed out first from San Diego Bay Harbor and Derek's yacht, *Silver Zephyr*, followed.

Jim was on the pier taking more pictures.

They agreed to stop at the deep water, Port of Ensenada, in Mexico on the Baja California Peninsula to rest the night and take time to check all the functions of their yacht. They would review any questions from War Julio and his crew about the motorboat. War Julio was invited for dinner with the Wrights. His wife, Janet, decided to stay home in Curacao with sick children.

Their chef knew War Julio was the owner of a large fishing business in Curacao, and he decided to make the California burrito for their meal. War Julio never ate the large burrito before. He was delighted to find the soft tortilla shell contained carne asada or beef filled with cheese, guacamole, and French fries. The fries were the key to the whole rolled mess. The chef double fried them. War Julio asked the chef if batter-fried fish might work well instead of the beef. Mango relish would be better also. Their chef agreed to try the burrito for the next meal but needed a week to perfect the dish. They drank double IPA beer. Dessert was flan with strawberries and the coffee was strong with a hint of chocolate.

Jess took the children down below for bed for the evening. Derek, War Julio, and Skid talked. War Julio wanted to know if Derek wanted to race the boats in the morning. Or they could set up mile points and whoever reached the location first received a marker like in poker. They could do three races. Derek laughed.

"How much is a marker?"

"A thousand sounds good," said War Julio.

Skid would judge the race and declare the winner. Skid thought he was being set up for a fall.

"Don't run over any ships in the area."

Now it was War Julio's turn to laugh, because Derek knew him.

"I will only run over the bad guys if they don't get out of my way in their puny boats."

The men turned in for the evening. Derek decided to wait until morning to tell Jess. He didn't want to ruin their night alone. She might be opposed to the races, thinking they were acting like boys instead of adults.

Next morning, the two ships raced. War Julio won the first round and Derek won the second race. The third race was too close to call. They agreed to table the third race when the ocean was calmer. Then War Julio cut in front of Derek's boat, so Derek had to catch up and cut across War Julio's bow.

War Julio called up Derek and said, "Truce. My captain is getting nervous."

Derek let War Julio take the lead.

Jess was also nervous. She told Derek no more racing the two ships, because there were children on board who needed good male role models.

Derek knew their children loved the racing scenarios but agreed with his wife to maintain peace. They could race with his new guided system, lighted, night-flying, and camera-equipped drones.

Every stopover, late in the evening, Derek, Skid, War Julio, and their captain on the yacht flew the drones in a game of war with acrobatics thrown in the mix. They used the cheaper drones that had pop out floats when they hit the water. One of the crew would fetch the downed drone and bring it back. They created their own games and added rules. Skid drew up the game information on the computer.

Skid told Jess they could market a new video game together. Jess thought that was great because it would pay for Derek's losses in the game. Skid gave Jess a wonderful idea to hire a photographer with night vision video who could follow the drones and capture the game.

Knowing Jess was very smart, Skid agreed totally with her to keep their project a secret from everyone. Jess wanted the video and their project be a complete surprise for Derek's birthday while they were in Curacao.

Skid would work to set the website up. He could teach Justine along the way about the website. It would be an education process, explaining to him everything he could. Justin was told to keep quiet about the website because it was a sample one. Jess would contact the lawyer about a new video game corporation and ask him to provide information to their accountant.

The captain and Skid were exempt from the drone game marker payments.

Currently, War Julio was in the lead five markers. The children were allowed on occasion to view the games. Derek taught Justin how to maneuver one of the cheaper drones until he could handle the expensive ones.

Things were calm, and they eventually could see Puerto Vallarta fast approaching on their radar screens. Derek was notified by his captain that the yacht was approaching Banderas Bay.

Derek shut his computer down. His secretary sent him the police update folder electronically and he received his reports from Tami Cortez and Rhonda White. Plans were moving forward on the police side and with Derek's team to catch criminals.

11 Meeting in Puerto Vallarta

ASSEMBLED AT THE meeting were War Julio Samba, Jess and Derek Wright, Skid Peters, Jim Michaels, Ara and Jack Jones, the Cortez brothers, other Miami cronies, and the San Francisco cronies. Their gang met on the *Silver Zephyr* in Puerto Vallarta. Mary Beth Michaels was taking care of the children.

Derek started the meeting. Sometimes the only way out of a situation was to bring everything down. The words were total shutdown. First, the police agencies would hit the high dollar businesses. Then the next one, and so on. Once everything was taken out of commission, the true criminals would appear. They could move in for the capture if possible. Or they would go in for the kill.

So, the question arose, "Who is on the list of high criminals? Do we choose the easy or the hard way to catch the bad guys? The police are willing to take the hard way which will require more brains and manpower."

Everyone around the table nodded. They agreed to select the hard way plan.

Derek took control of the meeting.

"First is finding the location of the chop shop that Minnow Surf owns and controls. The police are working that end, but I feel some of the Miami cronies can infiltrate that area better. The second is the marijuana and drugs which perhaps the Cortez brothers want to start chasing. The influx of marijuana plants into California this year is very high. The police find that the big-grow operations are usually outside the city in a wilderness type environment. The Drug Enforcement people will be involved there with the Cortez boys. The smaller robberies and pawn shops can be worked by Jim with the San Francisco cronies."

The groups around the table talked for a few minutes and Derek continued.

"Rhonda White is undercover already at the cousin, Randy Moore's nightclub in Los Angeles. So far, she has obtained little information other than Randy seems normal. Randy has sold his restaurants close to Minnow's turf, so it looks like he is distancing himself from the Green Stream gang. Rhonda is currently teaching Randy to skydive, developing a confidante relationship. One of the band members at the club is an undercover cop there on location to protect Rhonda."

Derek waited for comments and when no one spoke, he continued.

"Minnow's wife, Amy, seems to have moved out of their house into an apartment. Amy may also be distancing herself from trouble. Those two, Randy and Amy, might become allies for the police in the future. Randy is staying away from Amy and any relationship with her for the moment seems as a former friend. Later he did set Amy up financially with a beauty shop business which his wife frequents."

Jim poured Derek some more coffee from the carafe and went around the table.

"The tough part is there may be more trouble on the horizon. Two dead bodies of rival gang leaders were found. There is a high probability Minnow either killed them or did arrange the hit. Also, a local gun shop burned to the ground, the owner is missing, and we presume that the man is dead. All guns are missing and stolen serial numbers watched. The Bureau of Alcohol, Tobacco, Firearms and Explosives were watching this particular shop before the fire for illegal activity."

Jim set the pot down and his eyes lifted heavenward. He knew what was coming next.

"They believe a gun trafficker out of Miami named Matin Domingo is rolling stolen guns and ammunition through this particular shop and others. The types of guns are the normal handguns which were revolvers, pistols, semi-automatics and automatics. They also deal in long guns such as shotguns and sniper rifles with scopes. There are some small machine guns under fifty calibers. Some underwater firearms are also appearing in the underworld market. Then there appears to be people in Oregon who were arrested because they did carry guns with serial numbers from the now defunct shop."

Jim looked at Derek. "Is that all the trouble we have to deal with? We should check all the incoming ships for a container of voodoo dolls. That's usually where the con artists hide the drugs. Or maybe angels can help us."

Jack laughed and looked at Ara. She talked about the strange Miami man to him once. He nodded to her that she should divulge what she knew. She had lived in Miami.

Ara responded, "Or the bad guys park the sweet stuff in angel dolls which belong in angel containers. I did attend several parties at Domingo's estate while I lived in Miami. A remark that I overheard was strange to me but makes sense now. The visitors at Domingo's house party did make some similar comment to angel and to those descriptions about containers. I can possibly look at mug shots of people to see if I can identify them from those parties."

Derek brightened. "Angels are invisible. We should look for hidden containers within containers. Thanks, Ara. I will see if we can get a connection to Miami's police files. We may have to meet later at my office in Los Angeles."

"I will be glad to help."

Skid raised his hand. Derek urged him to take the floor.

"I suddenly remember something Amy said about a place in a small town called Searchlight, Nevada, off US Highway 95. It is the perfect place for a grow operation in a wilderness. I know she mentioned the place would have the potential for high money due to the barn structure's size. There also is the distance the pot travels. She did tell me that the farther the distance the drug travels, the higher the price received."

Derek encouraged Skid to keep talking.

"Minnow's grandparents did own an old house and large barn. Minnow didn't like to visit the place because nothing ever happened there. He was bored whenever he visited. The only importance was his grandfather grew some marihuana plants he secretly obtained. Minnow would have one of his men pick up a stash for him on occasion. The guy is a heavy smoker. Amy usually dreamt up names for things she didn't like and drew cartoons on napkins at the bar to entertain people. She wrote a name on a napkin for me so that Minnow wouldn't see it. It was the barn and the words: Nowhere Hideout. Seeing me smile at her joke, she wrote another word: Rigged. The nowhere is because it is so far away from any airport or super highway. The rigged part worried me a little. I didn't want to visit the barn and never did."

Derek said, "*Hideout and rigged*?"

"Yes, she emphasized rigged with her hands."

Jim sat down, and the Cortez brothers brightened. They liked to undo anything rigged. Derek noted their expressions.

"The police and agencies want to dead-end all their activities, rigged or otherwise, but also catch the major players by turning up the heat with added pressure."

Derek saw his wife raise her hand, "What is it, honey?"

Everyone looked at Jess, because Derek looked strange.

60

"What if the first target is wrong? Perhaps we should look at the one that's *no easy target*."

"And which one will be the no easy target?"

Jess explained, "The hideout makes perfect sense to check out first rather than the chop shop. If the place is rigged, then the drugs and marijuana should be there. Get inside without blowing the place, remove the major drugs, take pictures, and count the street value in money. Exit the place with all the minions out or captured, add heat, and blow the place. Of course, try to make it look like an accident."

The group at the table were interested. Jim sat down.

"It will be the first cannonball to fell Minnow's empire. Let the wind fan the flames like they did in our sunken ship treasure find. It can bring Minnow major loss of revenue immediately, and he will need to set up a new location fast. Minnow is lazy and possibly might ramp up the chop-shop or gun smuggling areas, thinking they are safe."

The Cortez brothers liked Jess and her comment about accident. It was part of their self-defense moves. They remembered Rio, the green-eyed prisoner, a wrong truck, and a bad turn. They smiled mischievously.

Everyone looked at Derek who got up and poured himself a glass of water.

"Thank you for the insight."

He knew Jess entered the game big time and was getting a step ahead of the bad guys, leading them to the fiery gates. Derek would have to race to keep up with her. He wished Dean Crain was there to help. Derek smiled because he was now the elected one to follow and protect her even more. He wondered briefly how she got her head start and then gave it up. His wife was too complicated and there was no manual to her logic. He was lucky to have figured out her code after she helped him. He saw Jim stand.

"The plan makes perfect sense. Finding the drugs should be the first target. The loss of income would be instant and make the guy wonder about who was after him," said Jim.

Derek smiled at Jim. He was also onboard. Jess reminded him of their sunken ship software scenario of revenge and destruction. Jess smiled back, glad her husband read her thoughts. Derek would check the ownership records to locate the property in Nevada.

"Thanks, everyone. Well, that's a wrap for today. Everyone is welcome to stay for cocktails and dinner. The chef made prawns and crab risotto with a light tossed salad and mango dressing. Let's relax for the evening and bring back the children."

Derek hit the number six calypso song on the stereo. Dean and War Julio's number seven would follow. Mary Beth would know to lead their children to the lounge. Derek poured Jess a scotch and kissed her a long kiss. He was so ready.

Jess's eyes said, "Later."

Derek laughed. It was a successful meeting. Their friends were valuable. "This whole set could work."

"Yes, my sweet husband."

There was no need for further discussion. They were on the same team which was always to catch the players in their illegal games. There was no room in their space. Jess already considered them imprisoned. Derek considered them pieces of the earth, ash, specifically. He knew Dean would be hailing him in agreement. He could feel the yacht rock a little from a passing wave. Derek saluted a memory.

12   Skydiving with Rhonda

RHONDA KNEW RANDY would like skydiving because he liked his fast sports car. She was a United States qualified instructor with over fifteen hundred jumps to her credit. Rhonda only jettisoned her main chute and pulled the reserve a few times.

They took a flight to Arizona. He experienced the wind tunnel. A company created the tunnel for tourists to experience the free fall a skydiver felt. They took lessons together. He could learn flying positions and basic acrobatic skills. He loved it and was very adept.

Next, she took him on a tandem jump close to Elsinore, California, after teaching him safety basics and how to land. She made him buy comfortable clothing with no belts and support shoes to lessen any ankle fractures.

They suited up at the skydiving school and were in the airplane. Rhonda checked her altimeter and they were close to twelve thousand five hundred feet. Per visual flight rules, there could be no clouds nor aircraft in the area. The wind was nominal on the day of their jump.

The pilot told her to get ready and the plane door opened.

Exiting the plane, they were in freefall mode for a minute traveling approximately one-hundred-twenty-miles per hour or two-hundred-feet-per-second before the outer canopy opened.

Randy didn't say anything, and Rhonda figured he was speechless. The first rush did that to everyone. It was part of the pure adrenalin thrill package. She felt him adjust his arm, so she knew he was still alive.

She started talking to him about how she was controlling the direction of their canopy to their specific landing location. She had shown him earlier their exit area from the plane and their final target landing area. Once they landed, she considered his eyes and knew he was on skydive high. Randy signed up for lessons that day with Rhonda as his instructor. Later she helped him select and purchase his own equipment and gear. He would have to let his wife Sandra know about the lessons and his new hobby.

Rhonda told him she was pleased to be his expert instructor. Every week, they went skydiving together, building Randy's flight hours until he could pass the test to fly solo. Randy almost forgot about Minnow and the disastrous storm headed his way. In the meantime, he was getting lost in the fun of the skydiving world and making new friends who stopped by his nightclub on occasion.

The band music was the best and the drinks mostly were on Randy who ordered massive pizza deliveries. Randy installed a high-end popcorn machine, because the young people liked the stuff. He bought salted peanuts, too. Every table received a basket of each.

The floor became a mess, but no one seemed to care. On weekends, the place was hopping. He needed to hire more bartenders and waitresses. His nightclub became the newest hot spot in town featured by the local news. The dance floor was always packed. Randy was making good money which pleased him. He was also becoming a celebrity asked to speak at local clubs about his successful businesses.

Sandra was in her element talking on the local television stations promoting her husband's business and excellent restaurant food. She met a few celebrities and dignitaries. Later she would help promote Amy and the products she was selling. Her friends would want to enjoy themselves next to a society wonder woman. Sandra encouraged her female companions to spread the word which they did.

Amy's beauty shop became the talk of the town. Even Amy was surprised regarding the increase in revenue in her shop business. That was when Amy started working on her dream for the future. A ripple of strength began the flood of ideas that influenced her decisions. She would later approach Randy about her plans. She trusted his business savvy.

13   Amy and Sandra

RANDY SPENT MONEY promoting Amy's new beauty shop and helping her hire qualified beauticians. She stocked high-end shampoo and hair products. The hair booths offered some semblance of professional privacy.

Sandra tried Amy's Beauty Shop, because Randy told her about this famous hairdresser he helped bring on board. The hairdresser wanted to leave cold New York for healthy sunshine. Sandra needed her hair to look beautiful always. The hairdresser was a master artist with Sandra's thick hair.

At first, the two women were cool to each other, except eventually the freezing atmosphere started to thaw. The two women had known each other for a long time. Both knew about the other or rather, only what Randy chose to divulge. That lack of information told the women everything. They started sharing their stories about shopping and dress designers. Amy wanted to buy nicer clothes and Sandra always looked excellent.

Sandra started to like Amy and vice versa. She knew Amy received a raw deal marrying Minnow when she was younger. Sandra helped Amy by getting her friends to try the beauty shop.

Every now and then Sandra would see Minnow arrive at the beauty shop. Minnow would look at Sandra and look away. A long time ago he asked Sandra for a date before she met Randy. She told him that he could take a hike somewhere near the Challenger Deep section in the Mariana Trench and live with the sponges.

Minnow frowned as he didn't have a clue where the Mary Ann place existed, but it didn't sound very hopeful that Sandra wanted to go out with him. Sandra should have said three words, deep dark oblivion, and then he might have understood. Sandra knew he wouldn't be able to look up the location of the Mariana Islands in the western Pacific Ocean, because he couldn't spell either one.

Amy would take Minnow outside the front of the beauty shop where they argued. Minnow wanted Amy to return to their house and marriage. Amy would shake her head and stomp back into the shop. She would lock the door and he couldn't come back inside. Then Minnow would leave.

Sandra gave Amy points for finally being smart. She didn't like the little creep either. The man was part of the wasteland she never went to visit.

The only problem, Minnow kept returning to the beauty shop trying to convince Amy. He refused to give up. He knew she would return. He needed lots of money, because it was what worked for him in the past. Besides, she always forgave him and came back. They were a forever-type of couple in his brain. He wasn't ready to let her go.

One-time Sandra was at the beauty shop and Minnow shoved Amy hard into the counter after a heated argument inside the shop. Amy clutched her side. Sandra stopped her hair dryer, lifted the lid, and moved fast in front of Minnow. She held her purse high in his face, like a heat-seeking weapon.

Minnow groaned, "Oh, no."

"If you don't leave the shop right now and go directly to the line for the high-dive cliff contest happening at the Trench, I'm going to take my tiny pocket pistol with the accurate laser light out of my large designer, beautiful red purse. I'll fire the pistol where I know it can change you to Shorty. I want to advise you also of the existence of six heavily-leaded bullets left in the magazine, because I only used one of the pretty copper tipped bullets at the man's tire on the freeway today. He cut in front of me and pissed me off. He gave me the finger one time too many. I did hate to waste that pretty copper projectile."

Minnow didn't know what to say.

"I don't like the color of the lead bullets left in my gun, so these bullets are real dispensable. Pushing Amy and hurting her pisses me and every woman on the planet off at least two times too many. Or maybe five times. I will let the fiery, awaiting ugly bullets be the judge and jury. Do you understand?"

Minnow didn't know if Sandra kept her gun in her purse or not. She could be bluffing. He knew she beat his boys every time in a game of poker. Sandra also would tell the gang the most fantastic stories about semi-automatics made with a mammoth ivory outside design. Minnow knew that wasn't right. The material was supposed to be elephant ivory. Mammoths were dead for years. He didn't know they found their buried tusk in Seattle. He obviously never read gun magazines. However, Sandra did.

He still didn't get her comments about the Trench. He thought it might be in the sea where sponge lived. Or was she talking about that loofah sponge plant in Florida. That plant was more connected with the Mary Ann name. He bet the place was a spa somewhere. He shook his head and focused on her moving purse. Minnow couldn't see through the heavy leather. He knew where she would aim the gun with her fiery bullets. But, did she have a gun? That was still the question.

All the women in the beauty shop were standing with their hands on their hips staring at Minnow hoping to see some more of Sandra's action.

Minnow figured he was outnumbered.

"All right, put the darn purse down. I'm leaving but I'm going because I want to. You don't scare me with your strange English. You and the other women should go home. That's where you belong."

He decided to leave quietly this time and fast. The women in the shop looked at him with despicable disdain after his last remark. He would keep his revolver close by in the future. The heavy artillery would be on his bike.

Amy knew Sandra was tough, but she was impressed today with Randy's wife. She saw the other women in the shop come to her defense and appreciated their support. There would be free conditioner and oil treatments in their future.

Amy needed to stand up for herself. She asked Sandra to keep the episode in the shop from Randy. Sandra told Amy she would keep quiet. She would only do it this one time. Amy understood. Her husband, Minnow, crossed the line again. Later, Sandra wished she mentioned the shoving abuse problem to her husband. Things could have been avoided.

The women in the beauty shop went about their business. The episode was quickly forgotten.

One of the women's brother in the shop was a skydiver. When she asked her name, Sandra told her and said her husband was also taking skydiving lessons. The woman knew Randy and asked about the woman, Rhonda, who seemed to always be with him. Sandra explained that she was an employee and skydive instructor.

Amy overheard the conversation and would tell Minnow about Randy's activities. She wondered about Rhonda, because she met her once at the nightclub. The person seemed to be entering Randy's life at all sorts of excitement levels. She was told by one of the band members that Rhonda was also a good dancer and once worked in a burlesque movie.

Amy wasn't sure she should tell Sandra. She knew Randy was no fool, but sometimes temptation and trouble sat on a person's doorstep. Her loyalty was currently with Randy. Amy didn't know that trouble was near her doorstep. Desperation would enter the picture.

14 Minnow's Drug Business

HIS DRUG AND marijuana business were booming this summer, so Minnow ordered a huge supply from Domingo. He told his Green Stream Nevada crew to make more room in their storage facility in Searchlight and to push sales on the current inventory.

He would be out of the office to acquire his new black limousine from the car dealer. Minnow was picking up his new suit and would get some expensive shoes. He stopped at a high-end store and selected new aviator sunglasses. They made him feel cool. He thought about buying a new motorcycle. He wanted to impress Amy. He must also impress his new partner, Domingo. He would appear like Randy did to the world, entrepreneurial.

Minnow's ego was flying high. He was so involved with himself that he forgot his parole officer meeting. He drove at a high rate of speed to the meeting and arrived an hour late. A highway patrolman stopped him and gave him a speeding ticket. Minnow was thrilled, because he could use the ticket as an excuse with the parole officer. He smudged the time on the ticket making a small hole in the paper.

His business entity in Searchlight was listed as an organic fertilizer company, and they brought a half truck load of organic fertilizer into the first floor of the barn in case anyone was nosy and looked inside when the doors were open. The place was surrounded by barbed wire and electrified fencing with a metal cattle gate. There was a small sign with the business name and a large Keep Out sign on the gate and barn.

The large trap door and stairs led to the white painted basement. The white paint was to reflect the light from the overhead lamps. At night, a pile of hay was moved over the trap door. During the day, there were workers loading and unloading the drugs and marijuana.

The plants were in one room with their own grow lights with reflectors and watering system. There was a main room with long table and chairs where everything was repackaged into smaller sizes for resale purposes. Then there was another room with storage shelves where the completed products were kept.

These items were carefully catalogued as inventory and tracked when the inventory was sold.

The entire electrical system was upgraded. New security cameras fed to the leader's computers. A special mechanism was installed to blow the barn if the correct two sequences of codes were not used. Each sequence was six numbers. There was a reset button in case someone accidentally entered the wrong code. A person could start over only three times. The outside box was also locked. Only the leader and Minnow held a key and knew the codes. Their Nevada gang workers were paid cash.

Minnow stayed away from the grandfather's old homestead because he still hated the place and didn't want anyone to track him there. Plus, he was paranoid the police would arrive if he showed up. The business was placed in his Nevada leader's capable hands. The leader watched the business for him while he was in jail. The business was small during that time and the profit only paid the necessary costs.

Minnow never ran into any problems with the Nevada group and the money was his pure gold ticket, arriving every month like clockwork. He was excited to expand this profitable piece of his business even further. Minnow knew Randy was aware of the location of this business as was Amy. They were told ages ago to never talk about the business in Nevada.

The Miami Cortez brothers were hired by Derek's firm to help with the police investigation. The police cleared them to start surveillance. They would wait until six-thirty in the evening after the Nevada crew and leader left the complex. Their white van with orange stripe that read Roadwork Crew was parked with the orange grader, dump truck, and portable bathroom across the road.

There was a large pile of sand and roadway signs on the side. They dug out the two-large beige, dense tumbleweeds and put on beige coveralls with nylons over their head. Putting on their beige work shoes and gloves, they held the tumbleweeds as cover when the security camera swept their way.

They took pictures of the huge electrical box, wiring, cameras, lights, and the time of the camera swing. The electrical box had been increased for the required electricity to fuel the grow lights to feed the marijuana plants. Cortez used a small screw driver to open anything with a lock on it. He laughed at the cheap security system installed and thought this would be easy.

They used some of Jess's climbing gear to crawl up the side of the barn and take pictures through a small window of the first floor inside. They noticed the fresh straw and thought *old trick hiding grass over and under a trap door*. The boys also noticed air conditioners and extra new air vents under the roof ridge and top of barn. The water pipe probably led to a deep well. There also was a large generator in case of power failure.

Cortez stopped and photographed a familiar leaf. He took out the plastic bag and put the green leaf inside along with a little straw. The plant leaf was outside the main door near the building sign. Cortez had smelled it. He smiled at his brother and nodded it was time to leave their spy location.

Arriving back at the van, they went back to their motel room to send Derek the information and photos. He included the picture of the plant inside the police specimen bag. Some words were included in his note to Derek about probable cause in criminal court and if not, at least a warrant.

Derek received the files and smiled. He sent them to his superiors to forward to the agencies that would set up the retrieval of illegal drugs and the blowing device for Project Easy Target. Derek sent the Cortez brothers a note he would give them the message when it was okay to check out from the motel, and they could go to another job.

Cortez and his brother were to place the tumbleweeds in the ditches on both sides of the road. It would look real on the leader's security pictures that the weeds blew into the area. The boys waited at the motel and after the takeout was over, they would drive back to Los Angeles to Derek's office where his secretary would pass the collected specimen bag to the police.

15   Police Takeout

WITHIN A WEEK, the police and other agencies were ready. Also, the large shipment of drugs arrived from Domingo and were stored on the first floor. The workers found it was easier to unload them there.

The bomb squad brought their robot in case there was a second trigger. Derek didn't think there would be one because he didn't think Minnow was that sophisticated. But it was better to be safe. Derek would let them handle everything and he would stay on his yacht.

The Nevada leader lived twenty minutes away from the drug and marijuana complex. The police would use tire puncture tracks to slow him down for arrest. They felt confident the names and addresses of the other Nevada gang were on his computer. Unfortunately for the police, the gang information was stored in the leader's brain which they were unable to crack and still be legal about it.

The plan was to unhook the security system, disable bomb wires, and send in the robot. Next swift removal of the larger quantity bags was the plan. The police were amazed the drugs were on the first floor, and realized they trapped a huge shipment. The shipment wasn't on the pictures the Cortez brothers took inside the barn the prior day.

They recalculated the inventory price of the drugs for their new report. The bad guys hadn't seen them coming.

Smaller bags of the drugs would be removed, then the marijuana bags. Next, the larger marijuana plants. The smaller vegetative-state marijuana plants would be the last to load. The device would be set, and their trucks and men would leave with everything complete in twenty minutes.

The plan rolled exactly as designed except one part. The planned part: the leader was arrested and quickly hauled to a large city Nevada secure jail. The unplanned part: Derek received the call from their superiors. They didn't have the final approval to blow the private property building but was assured the approval would eventually come. They hoped the approval would finalize shortly.

The bomb people reconnected the wires the way they originally existed before the raid in case some of the other gang members arrived and knew the code. It would be a huge surprise for them to find the barn and basement empty except for a few broken branch leaves on the hard cement floor.

The police threw their half-eaten tuna sandwiches and potato chips on the ground outside which brought in the raccoons.

16   Coon Friendlies in the Area

DEREK INFORMED THE Cortez brothers the eradication team finished their bust except there was a hitch in plans to blow the building. Their team was disappointed by the wait. The drug bust was very high on street price and the police and other agencies were pleased.

"Tell your brother you both can leave the area after you've cleared things."

Cortez contacted his wife, Tami.

"Hi, doll, I want to let you know there is a situational delay in blowing the building, but we did see some coon friendlies in the area that can clear things."

"Didn't Derek say that you should clear things?"

"The conversation I had with Derek was very close to those words."

"Then my smart husband, you have your answer. Make it a clean sweep but don't disturb the wildlife," said Tami.

Cortez looked at his brother. "A clean sweep sounds brilliant to me. We won't disturb the wildlife too much. It possibly would be listed as an accident. If it doesn't clear things, then the police can take their shot whenever they're ready. Everybody wins, except you know who."

The older brother said, "The plan is doable. The friendlies look intelligent. Do we care if the other guy loses?"

Cortez replied, "Nope, we don't. Are the peanut butter and apples still in our police-purchased cooler?"

The older brother knew exactly what his younger brother was thinking. They played with the raccoons one time on vacation up north. They named them friendlies. "We have half a jar. Do you think they like the nuts?"

"We'll see. If not, we can always use the spun honey."

Friendly raccoons did find the peanut butter on the reopened punch code security entrance box. There also was peanut butter on the punch buttons. The older Cortez brother counted each time the raccoons hit the button. He lowered his night-vision binoculars. He had counted twelve pushes by the raccoons on the wrong numbers. It was time to get the raccoons out. Cortez threw the sliced apples on the ground by the cattle gate and the raccoons jumped off the box running to the sweet cider smell. The raccoons were chattering to each other. It was party time.

The Cortez brothers waited in their van and nothing happened. They gave up and drove their van towards LA. They were on the other side of town when the building blew in a fiery blaze from the added fertilizer packages on the first floor. The older Cortez brother was driving the car and removed a toy sheriff's badge from his pocket and showed it to his brother. Cortez knew he would have to buy his brother a beer.

His brother won the best joke of the week. The badge was so small, he hadn't even noticed it while they were on the job. Cortez thought they would head over to the nightclub to make sure Rhonda was all right.

Rhonda saw them walk into the nightclub and she started laughing, because she knew them from prior jobs with Derek. They made a turnaround to walk out and didn't. Rhonda dunked under the bar as she was laughing harder. She immediately opened their favorite bottled beer and put them on the counter with baskets of fresh peanuts and popcorn. His brother pocketed some peanuts to eat later.

All the residents of the small Nevada town came out to see the lit sky. The closest and larger fire trucks were some ways from the small town. By morning there was nothing, but a smoldering deep hole in the ground. Even the ashes smelled of marijuana. The residents didn't know the owner and didn't care. They went back to their normal lives.

No one told Minnow that he no longer owned an illegal business in Searchlight. He would realize there was a mistake when the Nevada leader didn't respond to his messages about a monthly check.

Minnow owed Domingo for the delivery. He scrambled to sell the last of the illegal guns and ammunition. He called the chop-shop leader to ramp up more thefts of luxury sports cars or anything worth a fortune, because Minnow needed money fast.

He wondered if he should go to Las Vegas and play poker, but decided their game was a hard one to cheat.

Minnow started sweating because the Miami guy wanted all cash upon delivery. Minnow knew Domingo's goods were received at his Nevada barn. He hopped on his new motorcycle and drove out Highway 95 to his ruin of a barn.

First, he would get depressed and then angry. The evil would start sliding the scale.

The police were already working to find the chop-shop, following every new sports car license plate on newly-installed temporary highway cameras. They stepped up any investigation of a stolen sports car and put the locations on a map and checked their cameras to the car's last known location. They set up the grid and looked-for patterns within neighborhoods and owners.

Many of the owners belonged to six different golf course communities. Their security guards were hired from two local companies. Their valet parking people were hired from two additional companies.

The San Francisco cronies were inserted at each golf club in various work capacities along with undercover police. The police forgot to investigate the weekend evening coat-check women. Later, they would correct their mistake.

17   Confrontation, Amy and Randy

LOOKING AT THE empty burned barn, Minnow saw two and a half million dollars in product gone which didn't count the marijuana live plants. The half million was his share. The rest was Domingo's share. The barn wasn't even insured. He didn't know where his Nevada gang leader and crew disappeared.

All he saw were some raccoons. Minnow threw his half-eaten sandwich on the ground disgusted by the loss of his business enterprise. The newspaper media that took pictures of the burned ground did the same thing with their sandwiches the week before as did some of the curious townspeople. The raccoons were getting fat.

He didn't believe the Nevada gang stole from him. They knew better to avoid his wrath. Thinking about the gang's lost revenue, they might be upset with him if he didn't create a new grow business elsewhere.

Minnow couldn't because he had no money.

"It is always a money problem for me. This disaster isn't my fault. Someone is to blame."

He started remembering people that knew about his business. He would need to contact Amy and Randy. He would have to do so cautiously, because he might need a loan. A loan would be a temporary solution.

Minnow went to Amy's shop first. She was out back getting into her car when Minnow blocked her vehicle with his motorcycle.

She stopped and looked at him. "What do you want now? The answer is still no. I'm not coming back. I already told you this piece of information."

Minnow knew she didn't know about Nevada, but he must ask her anyway. "Did you ever tell anyone about the Nevada complex?"

"No, I don't remember telling anyone. Why would I say anything about that location? I'm not fond of the place in Nevada. Who wants to be there when there is California? I am not sure if I could find it again. We drank too much beer the day you took me to see it. Then you did smoke marijuana and we got lost."

Minnow knew Amy hated minor highways and preferred at least a six-lane freeway to get where she was going or else she flew to her location. She didn't want to get stuck in some dirt-water town and hated getting lost that day in Nevada. He remembered her hair got wet from the rain. She had been pissed about it. She was always mad at him for some reason or other. Minnow decided not to tell her about the lost business.

"Do you have some extra cash I can borrow?"

Amy looked at the new bike and assumed he needed a temporary loan.

"I can temporarily loan you ten thousand dollars."

"That will be fine. I need the signed check immediately. Can you date it yesterday?"

"Sure."

Amy wrote him the check and handed it to him.

"Thanks, Amy. I do know how hard you work for your money and I'll pay you back."

Minnow drove to Randy's nightclub and entered through his closed office door. Randy was doing his books late at night as Sandra was out of town going to a new wonder spa hotel in San Francisco.

Randy saw Minnow's face and knew something was very off. "Welcome back to the nightclub. Do you require a drink?"

Minnow sat down in one of his soft guest chairs. Randy moved over to his private liquor stash and poured Minnow a strong glass of whiskey. Minnow sat there and drank the glass in one gulp. Randy brought the bottle back over to his desk and sat the expensive bottle in front of Minnow. He handed him the half-eaten basket of popcorn.

"Is it something to do with Amy? I try to help her out because she asks me. I will always do anything I can for her. I know the beauty shop business is doing well and she is enjoying the freedom."

"Will you just stop talking? Did you ever tell anyone about the Nevada complex?"

Randy looked Minnow directly in the eyes.

"I wouldn't talk with anyone about the place. It's a place I wiped out of my memory as insignificant."

Perhaps it was the two words, wipe out, that set Minnow in motion over the desk with his fists knocking a surprised Randy out of his cushy leather desk chair. He landed a swing into the jaw before Randy wrestled him to the ground. Randy had been a championship wrestler in college.

"I will only let go of you if you play nice."

The button under his desk triggered his security people who burst into the room with guns raised.

Minnow told him that he would sit down but needed another drink.

Randy poured him a second drink and put the bottle back in his liquor cabinet. Two drinks of his expensive stuff were more than he was willing to share. He waved to his security people that it was all right for them to leave. Randy used his white handkerchief to wipe the blood from his face.

"I need a high dollar loan."

"Well, you certainly took a strange route to ask a favor. Will fifty thousand, do it?"

"No, I need at least two million," sighed Minnow.

Randy gulped down his drink. He thought the man was joking.

"Explain to me why the excessive amount of money?"

"I purchased some goods from a high roller dude out of Miami which were delivered, except the Nevada complex has burned down. The high roller dude's stuff went up in the smoke besides my own. The barn is totaled."

"Well, the fix that you're in right now is major and I don't want to know anything about it. I can loan you five hundred thousand dollars, but that is it. There will be no more loans until this one is paid. You will pay me every cent with our standard interest. You will never ask me for another loan. Do you agree to the terms?"

Minnow shook his head, because the money would buy him some temporary time from Domingo's wrath. The amount wasn't enough. He wanted to complain but stopped when Randy hesitated with the ink pen in the air. It reminded him of Sandra's purse. The pen was red. Minnow rubbed his eyes.

Randy wrote him the check and Minnow left in a hurry. Rhonda saw the security people commotion and Minnow exit the building. She wondered what transpired.

Then Randy came out. "I'm leaving for the evening and will you please close the nightclub?"

Rhonda saw his concerned face. She said, "I can, no problem."

Randy drove to Amy's apartment and she let him into her room. She was surprised to see him and concerned about the cut on his jaw.

"Did Minnow hit you for money, too?"

"Yes, I gave him ten thousand dollars."

Randy went to her kitchen counter and wrote her a check for ten thousand dollars.

"Your loan to Minnow just passed to me for collection. I don't want you to have any future dealings with him, because I believe his world is burning down. Someone hit the Nevada location."

"Oh, my gosh. That's why he needed my money."

"Amy, this time it's very bad. Minnow just did a connection with some real cutthroat people from Miami. They are heavy rollers and into high stakes. They are out of Minnow's league. He doesn't have the brains for their type of business. I don't want you to get hurt in the crossfire."

"Staying away from Minnow is what I have been doing. I'm going to have to keep my doors locked. It's the only way to keep him out. I'll also not loan him any more money. My plans will need changing. Thanks for warning me. Did Minnow do the cut to your handsome face?"

She came close and touched his face. Amy's concern showed in her gentle hand and her eyes watered. She looked at his lips.

Randy lost it and kissed her. Then he left.

Amy thought about what Randy told her. She knew he was trying to protect her. She didn't want to go to jail in the future or deal with bad people. She would stay away from Minnow. Minnow could be a very dangerous person at times. She wouldn't know that Minnow took out a million-dollar life insurance policy. The policy was on her. His life was complicated and uncontrollable. Accidents happened when things slipped off center.

Amy put away the check Randy gave her. She would go to the bank in the morning. She suddenly remembered telling Skid Peters about the Nevada complex. Now, she was scared. She contacted Randy's lawyer and filed for divorce from Minnow. If Minnow knew this piece of information about Skid, he would get mad and kill her in a fit of rage. She wouldn't tell him about the napkin incident. She wouldn't tell Minnow about the impending divorce either because she needed to protect herself, too.

18 Checking Golf Courses

THE POLICE TRACKED all pricey vehicles to a specific grid area and there were six exclusive golf course neighborhoods within the coordinates. There were undercover police and the San Francisco cronies were assigned to work with them. The cronies were friends of the Wrights. One San Francisco team, Allen Jackson and his son, Alex, were assigned to the police group monitoring the Grand Oak Golf Clubhouse and Restaurant.

The clubhouse and restaurant were always busy. The food was excellent and arrived at a person's table quickly. The restaurant overlooked part of the fairway with both indoor and outdoor seating. There were heaters and a large fireplace outside so people could stay and enjoy themselves during the cooler months.

They were told to specifically monitor the valet car employees from the two different companies. Derek's two men were assigned their jobs. The father was the person who contacted taxis for their guests and helped them in and out of the vehicle. The son was the person who worked at the front desk and received any special deliveries. There was a relief person if they needed to immediately leave. Their white van was out front which contained computers connected to the police and high-powered binoculars for day and night.

The father noticed the employee, Henri Harper, who wore an expensive ring and watch. He nodded to Alex to watch him. Alex also noticed the pretty coat-check girls on the weekends and he would stop to talk with them. He walked past their window when he saw Sybil with a vehicle ticket in her hand which she slipped into her pocket and hung up the guest's jacket.

Alex spoke into his hidden microphone in his collar to his dad that he thought something was going down with the coat-check Sybil girl and a valet ticket. He saw her duck down under the counter after taking the ticket, stand up, and put the ticket back in the person's jacket.

Sybil was supposed to lift the person's wallet while helping remove the guest's coat, but she was lazy. She was supposed to get the address, so the other women could steal the car from their home. Then she was to have her relief person turn in the wallet to the Clubhouse Lost and Found. But the stolen vehicle operation was stepped up by her boss. Sybil knew a quicker way of doing things.

Allen was out front when the guest arrived in a pricey yellow sports car. He relayed the information back to his son.

Sybil went off duty and went outside to talk with Henri who also finished his shift. Both walked together to the back of the building where the valet vehicles were parked.

The Jacksons called their relief people and they hiked it out to the van. Driving down the road a way to wait for the yellow sports car, they decided. They hadn't contacted the police yet because the computer was slowly powering up.

It wasn't long before Sybil came driving along the road inside the pretty shiny stolen sports car. The undercover police were contacted to pick up the tail. They were a couple miles away. Sybil saw the white van and became worried. When it suddenly turned out of her view, she relaxed.

The undercover police boys were tailing her, relaying the cross streets back to everyone.

The Jacksons were tailing the police when the sports car turned off the freeway down an apartment and residential housing area. A cement truck blocked part of the road as Sybil went around the truck. A second crew truck came through from the opposite direction blocking the police briefly. The sports car disappeared.

The police noticed an apartment complex with a garage and figured the stolen vehicle was there.

The Jacksons pulled over in the same residential neighborhood a few blocks away. Alex looked over at the bridge a block away and a tow truck was pulling the yellow sports car. There was a name on the tow truck which Alex tried to read, but the dirt was too much, and the license plate was removed.

Allen gave the limited information to the police vehicle who raced to an open area containing twelve warehouses. They weren't sure which warehouse to search so they waited until backup arrived.

The yellow sports car disappeared in a residential garage for later pickup. A delivery would take place via a heavy truck with a drivable ramp which brought the sports car to the chop-shop.

The operation was fast and smooth. The thieves' confidence rose. The police lost the car.

19   Grand Oak Clubhouse Plan

NOTHING WAS FOUND at the twelve warehouses except a few illegals who were quickly deported. The police decided to lay their trap on the two known thieves, Sybil and Henri.

A supped-up red sports car with expensive silver rimmed wheel covers pulled under the canopied circular driveway of the clubhouse. A hired, handsome actor exited the vehicle and handed the precious keys to Henri who promptly gave him the ticket which the actor placed in his double-breasted navy jacket. The actor didn't leave the jacket with Sybil but went into the restaurant.

Sybil contacted her partner in the restaurant who promptly spilled salad on the actor's jacket and removed it to be gently spot-cleaned. Jane delivered the coat to Sybil who lifted the valet ticket like she did before. The jacket was quickly spot-cleaned by Jane and returned to the actor in the restaurant.

Alex relayed the information to his father who notified the police of the third thief.

Soon, the red sports car left the clubhouse drive and traveled down the road for the police to easily monitor via the tracking device. Their entire team was monitoring the tracking to a residential area, hookup to tow truck, over the same bridge, and into the same residential garage as before. Two hours passed while the police waited for the red car to move from the residential garage.

Another undercover police followed the tow truck that stopped at a hamburger place.

The same heavy truck used before arrived back at the house and picked up the red sports car. The undercover police followed it to an older, former college that had instructed students in the auto body world. The business entity was listed as an Oil Recycling Shop. New white garage doors lifted for the heavy truck to deliver its stolen cargo.

The first set of police would arrest the tow truck driver shortly. Directions were given to move in with tear gas on the chop-shop building because they received the warrant to enter from the awaiting judge's administrator. Police were given information to arrest the three golf club employees.

When the smoke cleared, they found six half-dismantled vehicles in various stages. Parts were scattered on the floor looking like a local junkyard. The random mess would be sorted and catalogued for later resale to awaiting buyers in the underground world of con artists. The red sports car sat in an open area. The police were relieved until they noticed the driver door was missing, laying scratched, and ripped with a cutter around the door hinges. The people in the chop-shop had worked fast. There was no returning this vehicle to the car dealership's lease department.

Their books showed that they sometimes kept a car together for a high-priced rental client. The car was always painted with flat paint. They even provided a pickup and drop of the vehicle for these strange client deals. The money received was cash and only a phone number was used for the name. The phone information would reveal they were nonexistent numbers. Then the shop would tear the vehicle apart upon return.

There were thirteen car mechanics arrested, all women. Police trucks arrived to tow the partial vehicles and junk away. Another team arrived to strip the place of everything. A third team stayed to await the gang leader of the chop-shop to arrive, which they were told she did at the end of every day at six o'clock on the dot. She arrived promptly and was arrested.

The police let Derek's superiors know Phase Two was successfully completed with the help of his Jackson team. Derek's secretary was happy to send the file to him. She was awaiting the reports arrival due to a call from Allen Jackson.

When Minnow arrived several weeks later, because his funds hadn't arrived, he knew someone was conning him out of his businesses. The building was totally empty. It, however, hadn't been burned down. He thought that was part of a joke message aimed at him. Paranoia rolled into the mix. He wondered if there was a rival gang trying to overtake him which would add to the high winds of drama circling his life. He didn't know how to explain the lack funds for his next payment to Domingo. Minnow wasn't brave except maybe a little too slow in the brain to think about running.

20   Yacht at Panama Canal

THE CAPTAIN OF their yacht told Derek they would travel through the Panama Canal at approximately nine o'clock the next morning. Derek awakened at five o'clock and read the file from his secretary. He smiled and crawled back in bed with Jess.

Derek liked looking at her. She was his one and only forever. Meeting her changed his life massively. She kept telling him he should have run. He didn't ever want to run from her love. It was difficult at times, but so worth it. He was still tailing her, checking her secret dress design files on her computer. He found her surprise drone video game that Skid tried to hide.

Derek would have to act surprised about the game.

He started softly kissing her, sliding his body as close as he could to hers. She wore a soft blue silk nightie. She awakened with a bright smile in her gray-blue mist eyes knowing full well what he was up to this morning. It was a little early for romance, but she could feel his excitement. The canal was a tremendous boost of excitement. She welcomed his warm body to her.

Derek saw a beautiful flower in his bed. He remembered the champagne-colored new dress design which was filled with rhinestones that sparkled on her computer. Her notes on the dress said she wanted major sparkle, like diamonds. Yes, champagne and diamonds were her all the way. He made love to his excitingly beautiful wife. He would give her sparkle for sparkle in the early morning.

Derek moved off their bed and made Jess and himself a cup of coffee. She didn't drink much coffee. He questioned her about it.

Jess said, "Sometimes coffee doesn't taste right."

"Do you want some orange juice?"

"No, maybe later."

Derek left to take a shower. Jess didn't know why she was so tired lately. Breakfast didn't seem to appeal to her either.

Derek dressed for the day in shorts and crew neck shirt. Grabbing his loafers, he kissed her.

"I'm returning to the bridge and will be with the captain during part of the trip through the canal to make sure things go smoothly."

Skid, Jess, and the children would be on the high deck for part of the show. They studied about the canal in their education courses and were excited.

The canal took approximately six to eight hours to travel through the forty-eight miles from the Pacific side to the Atlantic Ocean. There were locks on each end of the fifteen-mile-long Gatun Lake. Water from the lake was necessary to operate the locks.

The United States purchased the canal from the French in 1904 during Teddy Roosevelt's presidency and later signed the Torrijos-Carter Treaties in 1977, transferring control of the canal to Panama in the year 2000.

Currently, Panama was building a third wider, two-lane canal, with locks to handle the mega ships or Panamax vessels. The maximum width for the vessels would be approximately one-hundred-sixty-feet by twelve-hundred-feet long and fifty-feet deep. The newer lanes would have basins allowing the canal to reuse sixty percent of the water in the canal. The maximum dead weight tonnage allowed on the new canal was around one-hundred-seventy-thousand which didn't include the weight of the ship. The new lanes would double the capacity the locks could handle in ship traffic. Their smaller vessel would pay a toll based on per net ton weight.

The children made colorful party hats to wear and Jess bought them sunglasses that read Panama. They waved to the workers at the locks and other ships as they passed. Skid had to corral the children below deck for a while to get them out of the sun.

Jess took her shower, got dressed, and put her makeup on. She ate some eggs and toast. Then she read her mail. She felt nauseous, ran to the bathroom, and upchucked everything. She sat down on the bed and thought she knew what was wrong. Jess was tired most of the time. It was a long time ago when she became this ill and fainted. Jess smiled, remembering the first episode, and the tall fuzzy baby giraffe.

She called Janet, War Julio's wife, and asked her to setup a doctor appointment and not say anything to anyone. Janet agreed. She knew how to keep secrets. There were lots of things that War Julio didn't know unless she wanted to share. Jess laughed at her conversation with Janet, because she felt better already. Dean Crain told her women kept things hidden. Here was a perfect example. Both women were sharing a secret.

She needed to make certain before disturbing her husband. Jess went top deck later to join everyone. Actress mode took over. There was plenty of time for good news once they reached Curacao. She was glad they decided to make the trip. Safety was very high in her thoughts. Curacao was a refuge from the storm coming. Or was it? She was unsure. Her emotions weren't clicking like normal. The hormones messed with her head.

21   Arrival in Curacao

DEREK'S CAPTAIN SLOWED to allow War Julio's crew time to reach War Julio's new fishing company docks and secure the motorboat. War Julio's captain let them know their yacht could proceed to the larger dock.

Once the ropes were tied and everything secured, Maggie and Skid were the first ones off the yacht. Maggie touched the ground where she was born. Maggie thought it was the very best dirt.

Janet and her children came onboard the yacht for a tour with War Julio and then they moved to view their new motorboat. Their five and four-year old children could select their rooms except the baby. War Julio was glad to see his wife and family again. He missed their chatter. Both ship's crews set their schedules for security while docked, including War Julio's additional security people. Both ships would be heavily guarded twenty-four-seven.

The Miami teams arrived and were staying at War Julio's condos. They would protect the Wrights while they were on shore. Tami knew about Jess's doctor appointment. She and Cortez would go with Janet and Jess for a suggested shopping expedition. Janet also kept her own security detail that always followed her. They were scheduled to go the next day so that War Julio and Derek could attend their meeting with the Curacao police.

101

The doctor sat with Jess and told her she was approximately eighteen weeks pregnant and he would prescribe some extra vitamins. He wanted her to take things easy and slow after her large party next week which everyone in town knew was happening. People saw the two ships arrive in the harbor.

Next, he asked her if there were any twins in either her or her husband's background. Jess was stunned by the question. The doctor thought there was a high possibility as he thought he heard two heartbeats. They should know for sure when she was further along, and the ultrasound was complete next month.

Jess knew there were no twins in her family. She would have to ask Derek. The doctor wanted her to start eating well. She knew that would be hard with the nausea. She also knew Derek was going to freak out about the pregnancy. He would worry even more about protecting her.

She told Janet and Tami and asked them to keep quiet until she could tell Derek which would be after the party. They both nodded agreement. The women were close friends who knew each other a long time. They hugged Jess. Janet told her she knew a wonderful maternity store where she could get cool stretchy clothes on the island. They headed to the store for shopping because Jess's slacks were tight.

She told the ladies about wanting to start a skin care line. Both women were thrilled. They needed a better skin care product and volunteered to be testers. All the women had a fun day and were enjoying themselves when they returned to the docks. They joined the men top deck on the Wright's yacht for cocktails.

Jess poured herself a glass of wine to avoid Derek making her a drink. She changed into one of her new stretchy pants and felt better. Feeling tired again, she sat down. Derek was busy playing host and didn't notice how quiet Jess was that evening. His meeting with the police was productive.

22   Party Plans in Curacao

THERE WAS PLENTY of room off the docks and ships to have the party on the ground. The crews arrived to set up the large white canopy tents, music stage, dance floor, tables and chairs and separate drink and buffet food tents. Special strings of lights would adorn the tents. Portable bathrooms were brought into the area.

The Mambo Steamrollers would play Caribbean music. Justin was singing two hard rock songs. Then he would sing a musical with eleven-and-a-half-year-old, Sami, and three-year-old, Maggie, dressed in tiger costumes. Ara helped create the dance routine and costumes. Her husband, Jack, found the fake tiger fur for the costumes, tiger noses, and whiskers. The Jones' daughter, Lis, was only two-and-a-half so Jack would be with her on the sidelines.

The zip line was set up for the girls to make an entrance onto the stage with the help of the Cortez brothers who would wear tiger suits. They would release the zip line and sit over the hookup equipment while the girls danced around them. Skid would wear a gold jacket tuxedo with black pants and would act as announcer for the music and events.

Ara worked with them on their dance routine. Smoke would fill the dance floor and large plants moved on pallets to look like a forest. The special lighting crew would use projectors as the scenes changed. The stage would be its own light show.

The party invitations contained a bar code which would be scanned for entrance and the cars would be tagged with a temporary sticker, so security would know not to tow them away. A drop-off area for limousines and taxis was made available. A special large parking area was set in one of the areas for the limousines and a party room for their drivers. Many of their guests would be dignitaries so there would be many vans and limousines on the premises.

War Julio installed high security fences around his fishing business with new upgraded security cameras. He kept his own onsite security people in their own room, always, with computers. The place was a veritable fortress when Derek checked everything out. Special diving crews and fishing boats would keep boaters away from the ships.

The elegantly dressed Jess and Derek robots would be displayed on the large center dock. Jess created a tiger headdress and mask for the robots. There was a chip which Derek could turn on with the remote and the robots moved back and forth to the number six, seven, and eight calypso songs on their yacht.

Derek would turn on the robot entertainment after the main stage. The robots would be returned to the yacht and placed top deck. The crew would later store them below after the party. At the end of number eight song, the fireworks barge would be notified to release the fireworks.

The food was barbeque with pork, steak tenderloins, salmon and chicken hot dogs. Side dishes were normal black beans with corn, coleslaw, tossed salad, bread buns and rolls, six barbeque sauces, potato chips, guacamole, cotton candy, a large gold-orange tiger cake within his forest, and compressed melons on sticks with dipped chocolate strawberries. The tables would be set with tiger lily displays and large ferns to bring a jungle feel to the inside tent space.

In the drink tent, there would be a carved tiger fountain with champagne and a full bar set up. There would be a mini-tiger cub fountain with punch for the children. Appetizers would be small plastic cups of shrimp, crab, or tuna. There would be cheese and bean dips, homemade crackers, and twelve-inch breadsticks.

The entire party was to honor Ara's tiger, Felidae. Ara was pleased when Jess told her the plans. The stage scenes would include pictures of Felidae and his offspring. The final fireworks would be tigers. It was to raise importance about saving a species.

Derek knew Jess created another wonderful annual party to honor their deceased friend, Dean Crain. She told Derek she tried to keep it simple this year. Derek laughed because there was nothing simple about Jess. Food and flowers leftover would be donated to charity by their hotel caterers. Their yacht chef and his team were relieved they weren't cooking for the evening. All stations and people were ready for the party.

Derek rechecked the hidden guns, scopes, cartridges, and ammunition on the boat. He checked everything on the helicopter. He asked war Julio to keep one of his night drones handy if they needed to use them. His captain and crew would have fast access to Derek's matching drone. Skid would monitor the helicopter if it was required.

Derek was getting an edgy feeling. Jess looked at Derek and felt the same way.

Jess rechecked her white dress with green ferns and was pleased she made the design empire waist. Her lower heels were tiger looking fake fur. She designed a matching dress for Sami and a different design for Ara and Maggie. Their shoes were the same. All the men would wear black tuxedos and white shirts with gold ties. Jess designed special pocket tiger print silk scarves for their male teams. The crony's wives would receive a gold tiger pin as their gifts this year.

Tami called Jess to let her know their close friend, Rhonda White, arrived in Curacao. Rhonda would bring her high-tech video equipment to capture the stage show. The two women were part of the team to watch the children.

Jess was excited because she wanted Rhonda to meet Skid and Maggie. She thought they would make a perfect match. Jess was good at matchmaking. She didn't tell Derek because he might slip the information to Skid. She knew how close they were at times in their male-bonding world.

23   Skid Saw Rhonda

CHECKING THE DANCE floor and completed stage for the party, she looked at the electrical cables. Skid saw her and came over.

"You must be the new security detail."

"Yes, I'm Rhonda White."

"I am glad to finally meet you. Tami talks about you all the time. I feel like I know you. We were so close in Dakar, Africa, but never in the same place."

"Then you must be Skid Peters, the diving expert. Tami talks about you, too."

"I notice there is no engagement or wedding ring. Are you dating anyone now?"

Rhonda was told by Tami to watch out for Skid as he sometimes liked to catch a person off guard. She thought, two can play. She would play along. Unsure if it was a serious question or he was teasing her, she said, "No, not really. I'm into nobody for the moment. It is all about Rhonda-baby and skydiving."

"Rhonda-baby, sounds like a good plan. What does a person do to accomplish that concept? I heard about your skydiving stunt. It must have been a spectacular landing."

"I've taken over a hundred classes to work on the enhanced image. It sure beats sitting around waiting for Mr. Perfect."

"That is an incredible number of classes. I hope you accomplish your objective. Were the classes for your job? What type of classes?"

"Let's see, there were more modeling classes, then dancing, and deep-sea diving. Oh, I forgot to mention the bomb class and flying lessons that led to a job as a pilot for a while on a jet, but I left the experience, because there were no guns. There was the machine gun and bazooka classes mixed in with martial arts jungle training to hunt down a suspect at night. I can sneak upon an elephant in the dark without spooking it away. I'm debating what class to take next. Do you have any suggestions or am I boring you to death?"

"No, you aren't even close to boring me. I'm not a normal guy. However, Tami told me about the man that broke your heart. It's hard for some guys to be perfect."

Rhonda was glad he picked up on her perfect word. Maybe she should throw that one out the door. She was afraid it was unrealistic.

"Yes, my superman wasn't good enough. I left when I found out there were four other women in his life. I hate being the fifth person. The number five is halfway to nowhere. I also did date a rocker named Wade for some time. He helped me get over the other guy and it was nice. However, our busy schedules didn't work either. We remain close friends. When I go on dates now, they develop a rash or something when I tell them about my current job. Those jobs are safe compared to the real ones I've completed in the past."

Skid was surprised at the name.

"You know Wade Brookston on an intimate level. You very much need to let Jess know because he is Justin's hero musician. Oh, and calling the ex-boyfriend superman is an oxymoronic statement like the expression: awful good. In other words, the man is absurd and not super at all. Or a person can look at the antonym of super which is inferior. As far as your current date guys, it probably was the mention of the bomb class which scared them off. However, I like explosives and old cannons."

Rhonda tried to suppress a laugh. "You are funny. Yes, my ex-boyfriend is a moron. What you did mention about my dates, I thought it was the bazooka that scared them off."

Skid smiled and knew this was going to be fun. "I also scare women off by my inability to focus on them. I'm still in shell shock from a relationship a long time ago."

Rhonda gently touched his arm. She knew about Stace who left him when she was pregnant with Maggie. Rhonda also knew about her accidental death.

"I hear from Tami that you know how to fly helicopters."

"Yes, it is part of my crash course series on taking one hundred classes. You forgot to ask me, and the answer is that I'm into nobody for the moment," remarked Skid.

Rhonda looked seriously at Skid. She knew he was exceptionally good.

"I'll talk with Jess about my friend, Wade."

"Do you want to give the dance floor an inspection?"

"There's no music," said Rhonda.

"Give me the coffee cup. Although we live in a satellite and cell phone world, we just need a little amplification."

Rhonda handed over the ceramic mug and he wiped it out with his handkerchief.

Placing the cell phone in the cup with the music turned on, he extended his hand to her. They danced, and he twirled her around several times before pulling her in close. They slow danced to the fast beat.

Rhonda was feeling so much better as was Skid.

"Would you like to meet after the Wright's party the next morning and have lunch with me? There are great restaurants here."

Rhonda smiled. "I would very much enjoy a lunch date. I can explain bomb wires."

Now it was Skid's turn to laugh. "I know you are trying to scare me off and it isn't working."

He walked her to the rental vehicle and lightly kissed her. He started to walk away, stopped, came back, grabbed her, and kissed Rhonda properly like he meant it. She returned to one of War Julio's condos lightheaded over their encounter. Skid knew he had lots of time. He hoped she did. She was what he was waiting for.

24   Randy's Parachute

MINNOW HEARD FROM his gang and there were no rival gangs in the Los Angeles area that owned superfunds to purchase a hit of destruction on his Nevada warehouse. There was only one person who pulled in that kind of money. Minnow needed to blame someone.

It was Randy who was destroying his business. Randy needed to disappear. Then he remembered something Amy told him. Minnow called his lead man and told him what needed to be done. Then he reluctantly left for his meeting with Domingo.

The temporary bartender saw Minnow's man come in and order a beer.

Rhonda had taken some days off to visit friends. Randy was coming in later. The bartender was distracted by some ladies who came into the bar. The man disappeared and easily opened Randy's door to his office and then left the building. The girls exited the bar also. The security guy returned from the bathroom and things appeared normal.

Randy arrived and went into his office. It was jump day. He would be jumping with a different instructor today with Rhonda gone. He wished she was there. Opening his pack, he laid things on the floor and saw the cut in the rope. Randy jumped back as if he were bitten by a snake.

Looking at the second pack, he thought the seal looked off. Randy made his decision. Opening the reserve chute, its rope was also tampered with. He went to the bar and poured himself a drink. He called his lead friend, Brake, to beat feet on his bike to the nightclub.

Canceling his jump for the day, Randy said, "It has come down to this bad scene. There is nothing between us anymore." He motioned Brake into his office. Brake looked at the parachute mess on the floor and cut ropes.

"Minnow?"

"I'm not sure, except Minnow is the only person currently pissed off at me. He wants more money and I refused. The amount of money I loaned him already is obscene."

"Do you want Minnow removed?"

Randy paced his office. "Something did happen to trigger Minnow off. I need you to find out what that something is that created the madness."

"You are probably correct about the money. He's already blown through what you gave him. There was a strange Miami dude in town meeting with Minnow. I'll check immediately and let you know today." Brake left the bar and took several biker friends with him as cover.

Randy sat in his office a long time. He could thank Rhonda for his life. Her training helped. Then he rolled the packs up and put them in the closet. He called Amy to see if she saw or talked to Minnow recently.

"No, I did not. I did, however, file divorce papers with the lawyer."

"Does Minnow know about those facts?"

"No, I did file just recently."

"All right. You keep staying away from him."

Brake called Randy back.

"No one is talking. My group drove to Minnow's house and he isn't there. His motorcycle is missing. The limousine is in the garage."

"Keep trying to locate him. Bring him to the nightclub when the gang finds Minnow."

"Will do, boss. I will bring a rope. We can figure out later what to do with the rope."

Randy nodded. "The war has started. It is fueled by the down-slope Santa Ana winds. The pressure has cracked Minnow, turning him into the devil."

It was Brake's turn to reply except Randy had hung up. He knew the future was filled with fire and darkness. He would tell the gang.

Randy contacted his wife, Sandra, and told her if she wanted to visit her mother for two to three weeks, he thought it would be all right. Sandra started packing immediately. It was their code to each other that there was trouble brewing. He told her briefly the current state involving Minnow. He believed she would be upset, and it was better if he informed her first. Randy would know where to find his wife. She was going to her favorite spa.

25   Domingo and Minnow Deal

MATIN DOMINGO STARED at Minnow until he looked away. Minnow was surprised the man was small, only about five-feet tall with a hook to his large nose. The man's hair was wispy gray, but his skin was very tan. His eyes were dark with no visible color separation that he could see.

Domingo wore a huge diamond ring on his hand with a snake head. He wondered who gave the man the ring. It might be a gift from some evil lover of his. Domingo looked the type to date scary women. He knew his estate in Florida was an expensive home. This man was super rich. Super rich meant powerful. That was registering in Minnow's brain.

Looking again at the man's bodyguards, he started sweating. He knew their large frames carried the best in technical weaponry. He bet the bullets were super penetrating, too. Minnow knew Domingo owned his own personal jet. He tried to figure how the men could get their guns through security.

"Do you understand what a falcon can do?"

Minnow was confused by the question. He thought about birds for a moment. "Fly very fast."

Domingo twisted his ring. A woman gave it to him a long time ago. "And better yet, they eat their prey, especially the peregrine falcon. A prize bird that you should take lessons from. Go watch them in the wild to gain knowledge. For you, my friend, are in wild country now. Did I mention that I own two of this species in my home in Miami?"

Minnow squirmed in his chair and thought it was not a good time to take a leak. He saw the men's room, but was running a little late, so arrived at the meeting. He wished he had stopped anyway.

"The falcon is a master at coercion."

Minnow didn't know what the word meant, and his face was blank. The man talked like Sandra.

"Intimidation." Domingo had his bodyguard light the cigar. He puffed and watched the man in front of him. The overhead fan swirled the smoke downward.

Minnow shook his head. The smoke was stinging his eyes. He was familiar with this word.

Domingo already assessed Minnow's intelligence, but he needed someone to handle the Curacao exchange of drugs and guns. His man currently was in the hospital from a serious appendix operation. It was a simple task and he thought the man would be motivated to perform. He saw the man squirm again in the chair.

Domingo knew about the burned barn in Nevada. His people were very good at research. He knew his drugs were permanently lost. Marijuana lit up like a Christmas tree when fire touched it. It was a torch zone. Plus, he figured there probably was fertilizer as well, because it should have been stored in a separate facility. The man sitting in front of him was too cheap to install a fire sprinkler system which would have cost such a nominal amount of money. Nor was there any viable insurance on the building which could have been an even tinier expense. Domingo had a fair assessment of the man's net loss.

The quiet nature of the boss triggered his security people on high alert mode. They saw Domingo's anger in action before. Anything could and would happen shortly.

Domingo was glad the man was squirming in his chair. He thought it was from fear. Only thing was Domingo didn't know Minnow.

"You missed a payment that is due, and this is the sort of business transaction that causes problems. But I'm a wise businessman and extremely knowledgeable about every little inconsequential thing. My people know me as fair, to a point."

Domingo turned to his security people.

"Yes, boss."

"I know there are temporary stopovers. Another word is holdover. The peregrine does stopovers or holdovers to collect its thoughts and work on strategy. The falcon currently is not hungry. This happening is a good omen for my business partners. Do you understand?"

He didn't know that birds thought too much about strategy. Then his bodily urges hit him big time.

"Pardon me, but I really need to take a leak."

Domingo looked disgusted but motioned his man to follow Minnow. He quickly exited the room. Minnow returned and sat back down in the chair. Perhaps he should have really tried poker in Las Vegas. This scene was not fun.

"I will let you miss this payment totally in exchange for a job in Curacao. I need someone to oversee an incoming, covert shipment from Miami that will arrive in Curacao in a day or so. The weather in the ocean can cause a delay and we hope there is none. In any case, we need someone there. You will oversee the transfer from that oil tanker ship to another oil tanker ship. The shipment is inside one of the oil tanks in a hidden, cleverly designed compartment. There is a special design impressed in the metal where the release is located."

Domingo drew the design on hotel paper. Minnow looked at the feather shape of a peregrine falcon. Minnow frowned.

"In my business, the design is called angel which is a name of one of my falcons. Do you have any questions?"

Minnow shook his head. All he wanted to do was leave.

"Very good. Once the transfer is complete, then you can leave because I have hired people for the San Diego and Los Angeles deliveries. My crew in Curacao will help you with a place to stay on the outgoing ship in Curacao and any other items. There should be no difficulty. My crews do this routine operation many times over. The original shipment has come on a different type of ship from Sierra Leone, Africa. You certainly carry a passport?"

Minnow nodded.

"I believe you do understand the lucrative and complex nature of my business. I'm granting you an exceptional opportunity to succeed. The gifts I can grant you are huge. There possibly are luxury cars, expensive watches, vacations, and the like. But this will come later after your balance is fully paid. Yes, I can see this plan as advantageous for both of us."

Domingo was tired from delivering his long speech.

Minnow knew to nod one more time even though the bodyguard wore a smirk on his face. He wanted to attack the bodyguard but couldn't at this meeting. The bodyguard could easily be removed from the living. He knew how to do the perfect kill. Minnow would wait his turn.

Domingo saw the evil in Minnow's eyes. It was what he came here to see. He was excited to see the evil come to the surface. The man tried to hide the violent thing blossoming inside him.

Domingo quietly left the room to return to his posh estate in Florida.

One of the bodyguards handed Minnow a packet with an airline ticket, money, and a contact phone number when he reached his destination.

Minnow went to his bank to exchange his money and drove directly to the airport. His passport and a change of clothes were in a bag in his motorcycle case. He knew he was given another opportunity but worried about next month. Minnow didn't want to be eaten.

No thoughts entered his brain regarding his parole officer who told him not to leave the country. The parole officer was the least of his problems. He started getting scared and then thought about the riches Domingo told him would happen. Domingo forgot to tell him those riches would cost Minnow much more. Domingo was like the court system. He saw liquidated damages as his right to grant to someone or take away. The takeaway part was his favorite ruling.

Domingo was the greater con artist holding the reins of the chariot to hell.

26   Party in Curacao

MINNOW COMPLETED HIS transaction on the transfer of the goods from one oil tanker ship to another ship. All types of law enforcement agencies were involved tracking the ships every step of the way. Minnow's picture was caught by one of the agencies. They wanted to make sure they caught all players and terrorists involved.

The crew was talking about a large party a person called War Julio Samba was holding at his fishing docks in the harbor. The man bought a motorboat and his friends followed in their larger yacht from California.

Evidently, the Wrights were there for the party. Minnow's ears perked up. He found out the owners of the yacht were Jess and Derek Wright. There would be heavy security at the party because the people remembered their last year's fireworks display when they were in town. The police would be there to keep people away.

Minnow smiled and asked where he could rent a high-speed boat with divers and diving gear. Then he selected the large sniper gun with massive scope from the hidden part of the oil tanker ship. The bullets took a while to find.

Picking up a revolver, he rolled the cylinder. This gun was his favorite but not powerful enough. He put the handgun back. His eyes feasted on the rest of the weapons before he closed the specially designed container. Rolling the long gun in his dark gray bed blanket, he formulated his plan and escape.

XXXXXX

The guests arrived at the tented Wright and Samba dock party. They were highly entertained with music and tigers and fed extensively. The liquor and drink tents were where high conversation took place. Derek and Jess circulated among their friends and dignitaries solidifying their friendships. War Julio and Janet were the respected rich couple on their island of Curacao.

There was dancing, and Jess saw Skid on the dance floor with Rhonda with a happy face. She pointed the scene out to Derek. He was surprised.

Derek noticed Jess was tired and made her sit down for the robot performance. Usually she was so up when these events played out. He stayed close to her after the robot show, refusing to leave her side.

It was time for the fireworks. They gathered their children, Skid, and Maggie, heading for the bridge of their yacht for a better view. War Julio and Janet stayed with their guests.

The caterers told everyone it was last call for the party tents. They began clearing the food tent and eventually drink tent. The tents and everything else would be dismantled the next day. After the spectacular fireworks, the children went to bed.

Skid picked a new magazine from his drawer and sat down to read. Security gave them the all clear that the party guests left, and they completed their final sweep. The police and their boats exited the area.

Jess and Derek were on the top deck with the very aged bottle of expensive scotch.

"Thank you, honey, for the tiger cake. I never saw so many candles in my life. I very much do like the drone video game business you and Skid created for the joint venture for my birthday present. The party is, of course, the best one. Let's salute our friend."

"To our friend."

"Yes, to a sweet, darling, and a much-missed Dean."

Derek held his amazing wife in his arms. There were no more words necessary. They left the robots on the top deck, still dressed in costume, and went to their bedroom.

Ten minutes passed. Jess removed her gown and slipped on her robe. She must talk to Derek. He removed his jacket, tie, and cumber bund. He felt the helicopter keys in his pocket with his phone.

The blast from the powerful gun shattered the night. Derek instantly pulled out the loaded revolver from a hidden compartment and threw it to Jess. He grabbed the loaded powerful gun with super night scope and headed to the bridge. He aimed at the white power boat moving toward the harbor entrance and fired twice. One bullet at three figures and one at the back where he knew the engine was located. The man at the San Diego Yacht show talked extensively to him about the engine and gas tank on power boats.

Skid came flying out and ran to the helicopter and released the hold mechanisms. Skid got the helicopter fired up, and Derek climbed inside taking the controls. War Julio put his drone in the air following the white powerboat, and Derek's drone was behind flown by the yacht captain.

War Julio's fishing boat was cruising out from the docks at full speed. Derek contacted the police and gave them the location and the information about gunfire upon his yacht from unknown assailants. Skid took the gun firing two more shots at the speed boat that Derek was chasing in his helicopter.

They were approaching the Queen Juliana Bridge when a bullet took down War Julio's drone.

"Man, there goes ten-thousand-dollars in expensive gear."

Derek saw the police boats fast approaching.

"Pull my drone back and have one of the crew check on my wife."

Derek saw the white boat disappear under the bridge and thought he saw a black raft enter the water. He relayed the information to the police and hovered over until they captured the criminals.

"We have two divers in custody."

"Is either one wounded? No, both seem fine."

Derek was panicking. "There is a third diver. Of that I'm sure. I believe I wounded the man while I was on the ground. I had him close in my sights. No, I'm certain that I shot the man in the arm. Keep looking for the criminal, please."

Derek flew the helicopter with his spotlights on the shoreline trying to see any movement. He sent the police the possible picture of one of the suspects. Neither captured men matched the description. They would send out a description of the man the drone took to their people. They searched for an hour and Derek returned to his yacht to see Jess. The police would continue searching.

27   Report to Police

DEREK LANDED THE helicopter and Skid secured the craft while Derek ran the steps to get back to his family. Derek was pleased Skid started the helicopter which saved valuable time. He thanked Skid and wished they had nailed all of them.

The police were already onboard talking to Jess and War Julio. Derek pulled Jess into his arms and thought he was going to cry.

"I am unhurt. Janet has calmed our children and is with them downstairs."

Derek nodded and reluctantly let go of Jess. He looked at War Julio who nodded. Both men were angry and knew Minnow Surf would be taken out permanently. Derek turned to the awaiting officers and they stepped over to the damaged female robot whose head was missing.

Derek winced.

"My officers will turn in the information from War Julio and his wife. Also, I have your wife's statement and we did receive your voice transcripts from the helicopter loud and clear. The police captain will talk with you and War Julio in the early morning."

"Those are amazing lifelike robots. They sure fooled me when I stepped onboard. War Julio did show me the sophisticated drone and how everything is connected to your yachts and helicopters. He also explained the night vision cameras on both helicopters.

That is mighty super gear that I never did see before. We don't have this in our collection of weapons. I can hardly wait to tell the office about them. The huge long gun with super scope is registered per your wife. You own some mighty fancy guns. The spearfishing guns I did see were locked in a case downstairs. Those guns are more than adequate for any killer shark. My report can be completed this evening. Well, I will leave you unless there is anything you want to add."

Derek's dark brown eyes turned to the officer. The officer frowned.

"Guess not. Goodnight folks. I hope they catch the last creep who ditched in the water."

War Julio walked him off the yacht and called back the Miami team for extra security. Janet came up from the children and they exited the yacht, leaving Derek and Jess alone. Skid went down below to Maggie. The captain went back to his crew and posted guard duty. It was a familiar routine on Dean Crain's former boat and the Wrights'.

"I want to tuck in our children and will be back to our bedroom shortly. If there are too many questions, we'll talk with them together in the morning."

Jess nodded. She knew that the two of them were in this place before with the bad guys. She would wait.

Derek asked the captain to remove the robots and clean the mess so there was no trace for the children or anyone to see in the morning. He thanked his captain for his quick action with the drone. The bad guys were surprised by the high-tech objects tracking them. It still hadn't been enough.

28   Bullet Fallout

DEREK ENTERED THEIR bedroom and poured himself a drink. He hadn't drunk that much at their party. He wanted to be alert for any danger. It was time to let the police take over.

Jess sat down on their bed. She could see Derek was real angry. He kept running his hands through his brown hair which meant high stress. Jess waited for him to talk. Derek put the scoped long gun and revolver away. He would get the crew to clean them tomorrow and recheck them. He would also inspect everything.

He sat on their desk. Jess knew she was going to have to pull him out of this scene.

"Talk to me."

"I will. I need a few minutes."

Jess was so tired. She knew she needed to lay down soon. She rubbed her eyes and Derek noticed the movement.

"I'm sorry. I know you're tired. Should I let our conversation wait until morning? I don't want to keep you awake any longer."

"No, it's important we talk."

"I'm so angry with myself. I held the shot in my sight, ready to kill, and my training took over. I did move the shot to the side to maim. Now I'm afraid Minnow's escape will place him in another position. He will try again. If he hurts our family, I will never forgive myself."

129

Jess came over to Derek. "You are a good cowboy, but I'll join you next time. Together we'll bring our pearl-handled silver revolvers and heat-sinking missiles to catch the bad dude guy. We won't allow him near our children."

Derek looked at Jess and kissed her softly. It was what he needed. Her perspective on their situation was very steadying. "God, you're so funny when you try to cheer me up. I love you so much."

"I love you, too, but I must tell you. It is our something word."

Derek couldn't imagine where this was going. "Is there a dead body somewhere?"

Now Jess laughed remembering the body in Tomales Bay she stepped on and her call to Derek to save her.

"The something is about us."

Derek was alarmed, "Us, okay, spill it."

"I did find out two days ago, but I did save the something news for your birthday. I probably should have told you straight away but getting the party ready and dealing with people tired me. Your birthday party was so important to complete my plans. Plus, I never asked you about the somethings on your side of the family and my clothes are too tight. I went shopping in between all these party plans so I can get comfortable. I did delay our something news."

Derek knew she repeated the word something over three times. It was making him more nervous. He needed to calm her down.

"Honey, you are driving me a little crazy. Can you just give me a hint of the something?"

Jess took a deep breath. "I'm almost four months pregnant."

Derek slid to the ground off the desk. It was too much.

Jess knelt beside him getting as close as she could to her husband. She needed him.

"We tried so long, and nothing happened. I gave up."

"I know, and I gave up. It is over eleven years since Sami was born. But there is more something."

Derek sat next to her and held her hand.

"How can there be more?"

"The doctor thought he can hear two heartbeats. I'll need an ultrasound."

Derek laid his head in her lap. Jess touched her handsome, brave husband. She started singing his opera song trying to ease the shock.

Derek sat up and saw his tired wife. He gently picked her up and sat her on the bed. He helped her remove her robe and tucked her in. He kissed her one more time and went to remove his party clothes. When he came back, his wife was asleep. Climbing into their bed beside her, Derek held her all night. He lay there and made his decision to begin their journey a few days early to Miami to get her out of the area in case the creep was still around. Moving the yacht was more important now that there was something more happening in their life. The news was way more something.

131

Derek remembered what Dean told him once, "Use everything at a person's disposal, even the underground world, to catch the truly evil con artist." He thought of a plan and would call his superiors in the morning. Derek wouldn't know another plan was brewing and would fall in his lap. The game would change.

Derek checked on Jess one more time. He smiled before he finally fell asleep. He knew there were twins in his family. Derek never told her, thinking she might run away from him a third time. He couldn't risk it. Now she knew everything there was to know about him.

29   Oil Tanker Escape

MINNOW COULDN'T USE his airplane return ticket to Los Angeles now because the police would be all over the airport. He hadn't wanted to ride the stinky oil tanker ship back and thought there was a lesson in there that Domingo believed he should learn. Now here he was stuck onboard the awful thing.

He thought Derek recognized him. He crawled up the bank of the harbor and hotwired a vehicle to take him where the oil tanker was moored. He knew the ship schedule which was ready to leave promptly at three o'clock in the morning. He barely made it in time to get there for a ride back to America.

Quickly cutting a blanket Minnow found in the stolen car into strips, he tied them tightly around his arm to stop the bleeding. He hadn't planned on getting wounded either. Derek must have guns all over his pricey ship. He was surprised by the two night-tracking drones and how quickly he could get his helicopter in the air. Then the police boats arrived so fast which was unexpected. He would need to be more careful in the future.

Once on board the oil freighter, he remembered the high-powered gun left in the raft when he saw the police boats. The inventory to Domingo would be short. Minnow thought they would not miss the tiny mistake.

"What was one rifle and scope on a person's list? It is peanuts."

133

Minnow would be wrong again. He made a crew member sew his arm and clean the wound. Although the bullet creased his arm, he couldn't believe how it hurt. The crew member gave him some drugs to ease the pain. Minnow would become addicted to the painkiller before he exited the tanker ship. The addiction would increase the madness. It was only a matter of time when evil would mix with madness to create a volatile situation that was inescapable.

He thought about his shot at Jess Wright.

"The head blew off, but I didn't see any blood."

That was confusing to him. Everything happened so fast after the shot. He hadn't been prepared how fast the boat traveled and then the painful shot from Derek. He couldn't believe the other bullet hit the engine gas tank. The man must know boats. Next time he would plan better.

Minnow decided to get off the ship in San Diego. He knew a girl there who would deliver him to Los Angeles, so he could retrieve his bike. She would provide him other creature comforts that a man required. It would be a perfect place to hide.

He knew how to sneak into his house to get clean clothes. He would pick up his mail and then bike it to San Diego looking for Skid. He believed he was there and Minnow would find him. He wanted to ask Skid if Amy told him about the Nevada complex or chop-shop. If she did, he would kill him.

Then he would deal with Amy for her errors in judgment.

Minnow was in destruct zone. The wind began swirling and creating a dust storm which would hide him temporarily from capture. The tornado would keep people at bay, far away from him.

30   Oil Tanker Interception

THE DRUG, FIREARMS, and customs agencies coordinated the timing of the capture of illegal goods with the capture of players belonging to Matin Domingo. There were so many charges, witnesses, undercover agents, cell phone text messages, videos, and photographs, his lawyer told Domingo it would be impossible to get him out of jail ever.

He was being held without bond due to the nature of the crimes and the international problems. The capture toll of Domingo's people was very high. They included many well-known rich and poor people.

The ship's hidden cargo of guns, assault rifles, high powered scopes, submachine guns, ammunition, and drugs were found at the Los Angeles docks. His lawyer read the number of guns and type from the police list. Domingo knew one gun with scope was missing from the Curacao transfer.

He figured it was Minnow's fault. He set him up with the police. Therefore, Domingo put a hit out to find Minnow and eat him which really meant kill him with massive quantities of bullets. He thought jail would be a vacation for the stupid creep. Minnow tangled with the falcon and there would be fast descent upon its prey.

Domingo gave his Miami hit crew the pickup location in Los Angeles for the plastic guns and the license plate number of Minnow's limousine. He also told them about the Nevada gang and where Minnow told him they hung out. His lawyer sent them full payment. Minnow was to be found.

The police later would have a problem, because the African witnesses and informants disappeared along with all documentation regarding the African ship used in the transaction. Even the ship disappeared, probably buried in the deep ferry lane where divers never went to look for sunken ships.

Unknown to Minnow, the payment to Domingo was no longer required. He would make a grievous error in judgment that would create gang justice. He forgot about the gang vote which was going to also descend. There would be nowhere for him to escape, because there was another hit generated that no one knew existed.

Minnow moved up the coast from San Diego and looked at the expensive homes along the beaches around Laguna and Dana Point. He contemplated stealing jewelry and expensive watches. Then he could take them to the local pawn shop. He watched the expensive sports cars drive out of four car garages. Minnow gave up on those ideas because it would take too long to make one million dollars. The security was tight, and the alarms sophisticated.

Minnow was upset that he couldn't find Skid Peters, the alleged informant, anywhere. He basically was at zero with information. That made him madder because he knew Amy told Skid things. She talked a lot when she was drunk. He knew she ratted him out. Minnow grabbed more of his addictive pain drugs.

He decided to take a walk on this high sidewalk overlooking the ocean and walked by a fancy hotel. There were trainer people on the lawn with tethered birds. He moved closer and saw the peregrine falcon. He swallowed and ran back to his motorcycle. Upon arriving at his cheap motel room, Minnow sat on the bed and opened his packet of mail. He picked up a strange envelope and read the divorce summons regarding his marriage. He got drunk and decided the only solution was to kill Amy.

Evil and madness were finally one. The tornado was a runaway one. It was what Domingo saw in Minnow's eyes and wanted on his team.

31   Wright Family in Miami

WAR JULIO AND Janet were flying into Miami to meet Jess and Derek for a concert later in the week. Janet wanted to help Jess pick her gown. Janet made a call and dragged Tami Cortez along. She contacted the shop and ordered this special maternity gown with black and gold stretch lace. She knew Jess would love the gown. She wanted to buy her a splendiferous gown as a gift from them. Janet didn't want Jess to have any pre-baby blues about her figure.

Tami laughed, "I have never known our friend to be depressed any day. Her figure always looks good. She is the most upbeat person. You want to go shopping because this is your former turf. You don't fool me, but then, a present is a wonderful idea. Count me in, girl."

They disappeared shopping, and Jess loved the gown from them and many of the other maternity clothes in the store. She spent a wad. The girls took her to a new vegetarian restaurant and they drank juice for lunch with fabulous cold pasta salads.

The concert was a present for Justin's fifteenth birthday. The rock show Justin did in Curacao was rehearsal for this birthday gift. Rhonda called her ex-boyfriend, Wade, who would do anything for his former friend. Wade granted only her any favor she ever wanted from him, like forever. Rhonda told him she was thankful. Her friends were very special to her, including him. Wade was pleased she called.

Jess and Derek drove with Justin to the recording studio owned by the heavy rocker that was going to perform at the concert in Miami. Justin wondered about the recording studio as they waited for someone to arrive.

Suddenly, there was a flurry of activity and the rocker came into his studio. Taking off his sunglasses, Justin stood up and looked at his parents. Both nodded. Justin walked towards the man and hugged him. It was his favorite rocker on the face of the planet, Wade Brookston.

Wade stepped back, "Total surprise, huh, man?"

"Totally."

"Well, I understand you know perfectly two of my songs from watching the videos repeatedly, like a million or more times."

"Yes."

"Which one do you want to sing with me at the concert in Miami? I was told your parents bought the special section tickets for approximately twenty people and they also know my wonderful, very sexy friend, Rhonda. She is a super good woman which I was a fool to allow to leave my brilliant hemisphere."

Justin couldn't contain himself, he twirled around and started dancing the introduction to his favorite song, *Golden Girl*.

"That answers the question, definitely *Golden Girl*. Let's mix things a little bit from the video. I will do the first set twirl, only backwards. The second set twirl, you will do it backwards. The rest will be perfect to the video. Do you think you can perform with the change?"

"Absolutely."

"Mom and Dad, please take a seat in the audience."

A curtain automatically pulled back to reveal the audience cushy seats. Derek helped Jess to her seat.

"Let's pull the band into the set."

In walked the band who waved to Jess and Derek. They would meet them afterwards. They did, however, shake hands with Justin.

"Do you need a short break while the band warms up?"

"Yes, please."

The band gave their signal that they were ready. It was agreed, they would do the first and second twirl three times. Then they would do the entire routine all the way through three times. The rocker's people would video the last set and give Justine the tape to study to polish his game.

Justin calmed down upon his return and nodded to his parents. They knew their son was ready and confident in his ability to perform. He increased his swagger in dancing and voice tone when he performed in front of a live audience. Their son was a natural, having performed many times at their annual parties and for their friends. Jess and Derek made sure he was taught by the best instructors.

The final song set was completed. Wade looked at the Wrights.

"You must be proud. Your son is better than I am. Can you ask him to tone it down a little, so I don't look so bad, not to mention old?"

Justin laughed. The rocker came over to him and Justin held out his hand. The rocker hugged a surprised Justin. Wade said, "Friends."

"Absolutely."

The concert evening arrived. The song duo was a huge success with the audience going wild when they saw the backwards twirls which they knew were different from the original video. Wade invited his audience to sing the last two sets of the song. The audience was dancing in the aisles.

The rocker needed to cool his fans down with a sad song, switching the listed order for the concert with his band. The Wrights and their guests exited the concert hall before the last song and headed to the moored yacht birthday party for Justin. Their guests finally left the party. Jess and Derek were alone on the upper deck.

"Thanks, the concert for our son is a huge success. I'm afraid our son will never be the same."

"I think we did capture a pretty good idea which career our son will choose. Does that bother you, because you did want him to fight crime when he is older?"

"Not at all. There is always Sami or the twin girls that can fight the bad guys."

"You were disappointed then with the results of the ultrasound?"

"Never. I will be surrounded by women. Who doesn't want to do that? Life will be beautiful craziness."

"How crazy? A little crazy, a medium crazy, or super crazy?"

Derek picked Jess up and knew she was getting heavier.

Jess's eyes twinkled when she saw him struggling to carry her to their room. He finally put her down. He was getting too old for this.

32   Amy's Proposition

AMY DROVE TO the nightclub for a meeting with Randy. He hired a personal chef to cook for them. He informed Amy she must not eat anything until she arrived at the nightclub. She was surprised to see he remembered her favorite meal of veal with garlic mashed potatoes and green beans. She passed on the chocolate mousse which looked excellent. The chef was removing the dessert when Amy changed her mind and wanted to take dessert to go. Randy grinned.

"You look amazing."

"Yes, I'm working with a trainer to get in better shape."

"I know you want to talk about a future business proposition. I'm here to listen."

"I feel good about my shop and would like to find a location in a nice area in downtown Los Angeles for a second beauty shop. My ability to make a profit will increase with the second shop. I can fulfill my dream of being a rich, amazingly good-looking entrepreneur. I know it can work. What do you think? I might need a little help with financing but will pay you back."

Randy knew she could handle a second shop. He saw her confidence grow ever since she got away from Minnow. He was pleased with the transformation and knew he would always help her.

"I will ask my attorney to find you a real estate agent that handles the downtown office building lease listings. I believe you are more than ready to take the next step in becoming that type of entrepreneur. Do you want more wine?"

"No, I have stayed too long and must go. Thank you for being a good friend."

"Always. Don't forget your dessert."

She went to the door and he came over and lightly kissed her. "Goodnight, Amy." They were best friends. He could relax around her.

Rhonda saw Amy arrive and leave the nightclub. She also saw the chef and the meal paraphernalia and wondered what the meeting was about that evening. Randy would give her no information. She knew Randy liked Amy. He talked about her once after a skydive jump. He also talked about his wife, Sandra, who became a good friend of Amy's by encouraging her friends to try her beauty shop for their future appointments.

Amy met with the handsome, sensitive, intelligent, male real estate agent and quickly became close friends. She left Randy a phone message thanking him as the person was very nice. It was a long time since she met the nice members of society who were normal. Normal was where she was going the rest of her life. Then she left him a second message that her new guy liked her even though her past was weird. Amy knew she finally found love. She mentioned moving in together with the real estate guy in the future after her divorce finalized. She knew Randy and Sandra would like the dreamy guy.

33   Final Encounter

A WEEK AND a half later, Amy was late leaving her shop and walked outside the back of the beauty shop, locking the door. She turned and noticed the large light in the back was not lit. She saw the glass on the cement pavement. Opening her car door, she jumped. There stood Minnow's figure, and his motorcycle was blocking her vehicle.

"You are out in the darkness and have scared me by not announcing yourself. What is wrong with you? Oh, gosh, there must be some bad people who broke the light, or the light might have exploded from something. Kids are always playing ball in the back alley. I'll have to call the city to fix it."

Amy looked at Minnow waving papers in his hand. She was confused.

He held the divorce summons paper tightly in his hands. His fist almost closed over the center. She suddenly knew why he was here in front of her. He looked angry. Amy saw him weave and lean on her car.

"You are drunk. I don't have time for your nonsense. I'm tired and want you to move out of my way. Move, now!"

Minnow stopped her.

"You are talking about my nonsense. What do you call this ugly thing in my hand? Why do you do this to me without discussing an important event you have planned? You can't do this."

147

"I didn't do anything to you. We grew apart. Prison doesn't have an exactly bonding effect on a person. The time between us was too long and it was those locked doors. My life, our life shut down. There also is your current lack in husband skills on several levels. I can do this. I want better in my life."

"Better, like good old Randy." Minnow was steamed. He popped more pain pills in his mouth.

"No, I respect him and Sandra too much to go that route. Randy at least is trying to help me. It is something you aren't providing me. You've not been there. Your promises were fake. Fake, fake, fake. All you ever do is destroy things."

"You're a liar. You lied to me about everything. You lied about Skid. Your information to Skid destroyed my business. Skid is friends with cop people. You lied about Randy, too. He's not your friend. Randy is in love with his bartender and possibly you. Like maybe, you, now that you're cleaned up."

"Your destruction is your own tornado within. How many lies did you tell me? What about the Miami person you owed huge sums of money? Who does that type of business? Only criminals work with criminals. You are a bad person to be around. I don't want to go to jail again. You're the liar. Besides, I can't do this anymore. I did find someone else to love. He is a real nice realtor guy. You need to grow up and go away."

Amy didn't have anything more to say. This conversation with Minnow was going nowhere. She probably shouldn't have mentioned the other person in her life, but she wanted him to stop harassing her so much. It wasn't fair.

Minnow heard her last two sentences. One of them was resounding in his fogged brain. She said there was someone else. It was too much. He grabbed her and tried to kiss her. She pushed him away. He tried to kiss her again, and she hit him. He shoved her hard into the car door. She hit him again. Her muscles improved with her trainer's help. Amy was now extremely tired of Minnow's attempts to recover their lost marriage. He wasn't going to shove her anymore. Her car was her safety zone. She could lock the car doors and drive away.

She turned to get in her car.

He stumbled backward, withdrew the gun, and fired at close range.

She lay on the ground bleeding as he stood over her. She saw the evil madness in his eyes. Minnow threw his half smoked, hand rolled cigarette under her car. He calmly climbed onto his motorcycle, pushing it to the corner, before starting the engine.

Amy knew she lay dying. She touched the blood and raised her arm to the cement trying to draw the familiar signature. Her finger of blood starting the circle and upward swoop. Her finger stopped. She remembered the gift basket she requested her friend do for a future delivery. She told them to leave the delivery inside the porch. Amy smiled. Randy would miss her. Her friend would miss her and vice versa. Then she thought of her letter before she fell unconscious.

The morning would slowly arrive. The dream was so close, almost within reach.

34   Call to Derek

DEREK RECEIVED A call from his secretary to check the completed police report. He had previously talked with Jess on the cell phone. Jess, Skid, and the children were visiting the Miami zoo and would be gone several hours. Last week they went scuba diving in Key Largo and shell hunting.

Derek saw the title of the file and sat back in the desk chair. He knew the file was coming. This report was something major in their project. It was about Amy Surf. It was an unexpected turn for them.

He didn't know if he wanted to read the report. He read the details and knew it was her husband, Minnow, who shot the gun. Derek regretted that he hadn't taken the kill shot in Curacao. He couldn't because the attempted shot from Minnow was aimed toward a machine, a piece of property which was a robot.

Derek read the divorce completed three days ago, for Amy and Minnow Surf. Her new emergency contact was her business partner, Randy Moore. The report listed Randy's lawyer as her legal counsel. He knew Minnow left her behind her shop to die.

Calling his secretary, he thanked her for making his earlier flight reservations, and he would pick up return tickets later in the week at the airport.

He would need to interview Randy. He sent Tami a note. Rhonda wouldn't be surprised when he walked into the nightclub. He also gave her information regarding Amy Surf and the notice that the hunt would increase for the location of Minnow. Derek informed Tami that he would talk with Rhonda about the update after his arrival at the nightclub.

Next, he contacted Jim Michaels to see if he found information on locating Minnow. He gave him the new report regarding Amy. Jim wanted to drive out with Derek to the nightclub. He would wait in the bar and talk with Rhonda.

Then Derek wouldn't need to spend so much time interviewing her. Derek thought that was a good idea. He didn't want to blow her cover. Jim didn't want him to be around an explosive gang situation alone. Jim reminded Derek about gang rules, voting, and consequences.

Derek was familiar with the justice route with gangs. He was worried Randy may seek revenge and do something stupid. Derek needed Randy to come on board with the police to find Minnow.

He didn't know how to maneuver the discussion. He knew Randy may have already created his own agenda after he completed her funeral and final burial arrangements. From what Rhonda told him, the man was still in love with Amy as well as his wife. The only thing, Sandra, was the one married to Randy and sleeping with him.

Derek was unsure of whether the yacht should start the return trip to San Diego. They needed to start the journey soon. Jess wanted to deliver the twins with her doctor in San Diego. There was a high probability she would deliver early. Derek called the bridge to speak to the captain and contacted the chef.

The decision was made for the yacht to leave Miami in the morning. The food supplies were loaded, the tanks of fuel were full, and the balance of their crew would return to the yacht that evening. Derek asked the chef to prepare a simple meal for everyone, so they could retire early. The chef would make pizza and salad for Skid and the children. Derek asked that Jess should receive her special Caesar salad with fresh fruit on the side. She would want her favorite hot tea.

The minute Jess talked with Derek, she knew something was wrong. She went to their bedroom while the others ate their dinner. Derek told her the chef would bring her meal. The Wrights talked a long time about what transpired. Derek informed her of the private plan. She knew the plan would work.

Skid took the children below to watch television for a while, because Jess hadn't returned.

The captain came down and informed Skid of the yacht's plans to leave in the morning for San Diego. While Derek's plan was to stay in Los Angeles, the captain was asked to relay the news. Jess would talk with Skid in the morning.

Derek would try to meet back with the yacht on one of their stops. Skid knew Derek didn't know how long he was going to be gone. They started the children on their homework after the Miami skyline disappeared.

Skid met Jess in the lounge.

Jess looked contemplative.

Skid asked her, "What's wrong, Jess?"

"The problem is Amy Surf. She was shot behind her beauty shop in Los Angeles. The police are looking for Minnow as the highly questionable suspect in the shooting. He is the only suspect."

Skid sat there stunned. He thought about his relationship with Amy.

"What did she do to make her husband so mad? He must have flipped out. She doesn't deserve this type of fate. I hope the police catch him. What a creep?"

"Amy received her divorce from Minnow. He probably didn't know about the finalization which would null and void his million-dollar life insurance policy he recently took out on her."

Skid shook his head. He didn't understand people and their bad decisions.

Jess went to the bar and poured Skid his favorite drink. Skid sat there a long time. Jess sat with him. Finally, the children's chatter disturbed them. Skid excused himself and went below.

Jess told Derek the talk would be hard, and he would assume the worst. She knew Skid's tender heart. After Skid went to bed, Jess wished Rhonda were onboard the yacht to help with Skid's reaction. Rhonda was a vibrant, practical person with huge compassion also.

35 Skid's Invitation

SKID WAS THINKING the same thoughts as Jess. He needed a close friend. Life was passing him by. He wanted someone to hold and right now, there was only one person on his horizon. He remembered the feel of her in his arms dancing.

Calling Rhonda, Skid was relieved and happy to hear her voice again.

"Do you have time to talk five to ten minutes?"

"Yes, let me get the other bartender to cover for me and I'll go outside on my break."

Rhonda knew Skid wanted to talk about Amy.

"We didn't have enough time together in Curacao because the yacht left so fast. When I met you, and danced with you twice, I did feel major sparks flying. I haven't had those feelings for a very long time."

Rhonda was thrilled.

"I did feel the sparks also and wondered about you. You were a good listener for my explanation about bomb wires."

Encouraged by her teasing words, Skid told himself it was now or never.

"When this whole crappy business with Minnow is over, or sooner, can we get together anywhere or in San Diego to check our amazing feelings out? I'm thinking, you can stay at my house in San Diego for however long you like. I'm thinking you can stay a lifetime, because I know that I'm totally in love with you. When you think about what I just said, your mind goes, that is crazy because we didn't have sex yet. I believe that when we do make love, you'll really fall in love with me, the super great diver guy. What do you think?"

Rhonda was speechless, and she didn't know what to say.

"Are you always this straight forward with women?"

"Only the super beautiful ones."

"I will love to get together and stay with you anywhere or at your home in San Diego. We need to see about the sex part as the rest of you does look wonderful."

Now it was Skid's turn to be speechless.

"Our group at the nightclub were disheartened and sorry about Amy getting shot. I know you did care for her once."

"Thanks. I'm sending a massive bouquet of white daisies because they were her favorite. She wore this daisy-smelling cologne, too. Maggie did help pick the flowers online. I did mention to my daughter that flowers carry people to the angels in heaven. It's the fragrance that they love, too."

"That is a nice idea to plant in her mind. I'm attending the funeral and will look for the flowers."

"I must let you get back to work and will call you when I can."

"I'll wait for your calls. Good day super great diver guy."

"Good day, my super beautiful woman."

Rhonda went back into the nightclub walking on air.

She pulled up the clean wrack of shot glasses. Then she opened a new bottle of whiskey to have available because she thought the motorcycle gang would be arriving shortly to console Randy and discuss Amy's funeral. She would talk with Tami that evening for a more private report.

36   Derek Met Randy

DEREK'S BLACK AND very expensive sports car pulled next to Randy's sports car in the back of the nightclub. The joint took on a high and rich category to any patrons who happened to visit. The cars looked out of place to the exterior. Derek also noted the money put into the furnishings as he stepped inside. The place looked rustic on the outside but was expensive on the inside.

"Looks can be so deceiving. I see tasteful here."

"Isn't that the best way to describe this place. Joint doesn't apply. There's no bikini women, grungy bikers, or stripper poles. There isn't even a jukebox. Remember those things in the bars we used to frequent a long time ago. They had 45 RPM records on a moving disk. Those songs were real words, not repetitive gibberish. I loved to watch the machine flip those suckers, or rather records over, and put them back in their slot while song number 2 entered the sound system. It was the best part of the show and only cost a quarter. Nope, I'll have to retract my statement. The best was dancing with women on the wood floor in the joint. What was a draft beer, fifty-cents? Worth it every time. Oh, yeah, dancing was the best part," noted Jim.

Derek laughed and thought of his wife. She would love the stripper pole comment and fifty-cents.

His friend knew how to turn a tense situation into reality. Derek relaxed.

"I miss the slot machines and only three handlebars for tap beer. It was one of three major brands, unless you were in a small town. Then it was cheap, half-way cheap, and top-of-the-line cheap in the beer category. The liquor was debatable, most probably watered down."

Jim shook his head. He could see his partner chill out. It was what he intended in the talkative distraction zone. Jess told him to help Derek when he tensed up. He liked Derek's wife and would help whenever he could.

"There certainly wasn't any good amber beer back a century or so. Am I getting old? The new stuff scares me. Peanut butter beer, that stuff is real terrible. Yeah, miss those slots, too. I always won. They called me Master Jim."

Derek frowned as if he didn't believe him.

"It's true. I swear on my mother's grave."

Derek and Jim went into the bar area. Rhonda saw them on the road and was ready. Rhonda signaled the security person who ushered Derek to Randy's plush office. The wood and marble alone must have cost a small fortune. After the two left, Rhonda poured Jim a drink.

"Nice place and good liquor. What is a pretty girl like you doing in this nightclub when there is sunshine and the ocean waiting for you?"

"Thank you. Yes, I'm definitely living it up. I am glad you stopped by this place. We love seeing new customers. Doesn't this place look rich? However, I'm hoping to get some of the token California sunshine and Pacific blue ocean water soon. I carry a picture of the beach on my cell phone, just to remind me of fun."

Jim winked at her. He knew about Skid. Rhonda always thrived on an assignment. She gave him only a basket of the nuts. She knew Jim wasn't a fan of popcorn.

XXXXXX

Randy was looking out his window and turned around when Derek entered the room. Randy went to the beauty shop after the police disappeared and found Minnow's rolled cigarette under her wheel tire. He didn't want to believe Minnow could be so cruel. He nodded to his security person this visit from the police investigator was expected.

"My name is Derek Wright from Los Angeles working with the police regarding a friend of yours, Amy Surf."

"I recognized your face from celebrity pictures in the newspaper, but I don't believe we have met before. I do know why you are in my nightclub."

"Where were you the night Amy Surf was shot?"

Randy hadn't expected the question so soon. "Unfortunately, I was at my nightclub until one-thirty in the early morning hours. You can verify the information with my employees and security detail. I wish that I was on the scene last night to protect Amy.

The person wouldn't have been able to even move a finger after encountering me."

Derek knew that Randy wrestled in high school and college. He still looked fit and could possibly take a man down and out for some time.

"I will check shortly on the verification of your whereabouts. I'm sorry. Whenever a young woman is hurt and, in this case, it's bad. The person stood very close to her. She didn't have a chance at any defense when she was shot. Our theory is that she knew the person who approached."

Randy went to his bar and poured himself a drink. He motioned to Derek who shook his head that he didn't want one. He noticed the unshaved beard on Randy. Derek knew this scene with Randy would be hard. He could feel and see the man's pain.

"I want to show you some pictures of Amy at the scene. The police need help in apprehending the person. Besides the bullet, there is some bruising on her body. Would you look at the photographs?"

Randy held out his hand for the folder. He stood by his desk and went through the photographs. He quickly sat down and slid the paper pages to one photo. Randy couldn't believe what he saw.

Derek saw him hesitate. "Is there anything about the photos that can help us?"

Randy shook his head and slid the photograph folder back to Derek.

"No, there is nothing."

Derek told him how Minnow tried to kill his own wife in Curacao but shot their robot instead. Randy was no longer listening. Derek paused, and finally told Randy about the purchased million-dollar life insurance policy Minnow took out on his wife, Amy. Randy looked at Derek and blinked. His face looked grim. Then Randy turned, looked at nothing out his large window, and suddenly, asked Derek to leave. Randy had some business to attend to. The pictures revealed something.

Derek talked with Rhonda and the security team who verified their boss whereabouts on the night in question. Leaving the nightclub, Jim and Derek saw twenty motorcyclists on the private road. They moved to single file rotation to allow a heavy-set man to enter the lead position. Derek didn't see Minnow among them. He called Rhonda, who was surprised to receive the call.

"Motorcycles heading your way. Who is the lead cyclist?"

"I only know his name as Brake. He and Randy are tight. I do have a picture of the guy and I'll send it to your cell phone. Brake has always been shy and polite to me except I think he does help Randy somehow. They meet quite a bit. I believe Randy pays him, but I can't verify that piece of information. Brake looks up to Randy. Those are the only items I've noted."

"All right, I get it that you like the guy. Watch him for us. Try to get close and perhaps he'll reveal secret things. See if you can find out what the meeting is about today without causing attention."

"I will try."

Rhonda frowned over the information Jim provided earlier. Tami hadn't the authority to tell her. She would do her undercover job well.

Jim and Derek looked at each other while they were driving past the motorcyclists in his sports car. Both men said the word at the same time.

"Trouble."

There was a change in the air as they left Randy's place of business. A firestorm was brewing. The gang would be informed of the meeting between a Los Angeles investigator and Randy. It was about time for knowledge to flow and fill the cracks in the police case. It was what Derek hoped would occur. Derek was good at laying the groundwork. He nodded to Jim that their mission was accomplished. Jim already knew. His experience filled a lot of cracks, too. He had brought his gun and wore it under his shirt in case the meeting was a bust.

37 Motorcycle Gang Vote

BRAKE KNOCKED ON the office door and hugged Randy when he opened the door. Randy knew his next job would be tough. Brake moved to the side, silent and very quiet. No one spoke. They would let Randy take the lead. Brake was second in this room. Randy stepped aside and let the gang into the room. His glass of whiskey was half full. He filled it back to the top and asked them if they wanted anything to drink.

Brake held up his hand, halting those headed to Randy's small office bar. Brake knew how expensive the liquor was in this room. His group wouldn't appreciate the good stuff. He knew something was wrong. He still had some authority with the gang when Randy was down. He knew it was bad, way worse than he had figured. Randy was not right. But he had obtained information about Amy. The group would listen. They owed him and his boss that effort.

"The bikers will drink after the meeting. You can start. Please let us know what you have found about our friend."

The other bikers nodded, silent and polite. There was a hush over all of them. They waited.

Randy started to speak and stopped. His voice wasn't working. He looked at Brake who walked over closer to him. Brake stood beside him, tall and erect. Randy felt the confidence in his right-hand man. He needed to do this. It was important.

164

Randy cleared his throat. "Derek Wright, the Los Angeles investigator did visit me. We know why he came to my office. It was to check us out, especially me. However, he did show me valuable police information. He did this willingly."

"Is that the dude driving the fancy sports car that we passed on your road?"

"Yes, it was him."

The other bikers had seen the sports car and two men shapes in the vehicle.

"Wow, police work really pays well. His car must have cost as much as yours," stated Brake.

The others laughed. They knew expensive. Then, they became solemn again, noting Randy's distress. Brake moved behind Randy.

"Mr. Wright owns many other enterprises. He can afford expensive."

"I know that fact," said Brake. He had searched the name out on his computer and knew the man's wife was into fashion. This information was irrelevant to their meeting.

"I think the group would like to hear what information was presented."

Randy slowly came back into his office space. He had visibly paged out. He would thank Brake later.

"The police want help with information and need to know Minnow's location. That is why Derek did share police photos and something else pertinent with me. He believed I could find Minnow. The police are at a loss."

"The gang doesn't help police and we haven't any information ourselves where the rat is currently hiding," said Brake. The others were in total agreement to those facts. No one saw Minnow. He wasn't in the area. They looked at Randy.

"I went to the scene after the police left. There was a hand-rolled cigarette butt under Amy's car tire that I found. It was stuck good under her tires. I smelled the butt and it was the same as Minnow smoked. Hand-rolled cigarettes are an anomaly. Few people use those methods. There are e-cigarettes, a highly different way of smoking. He was addicted to the tobacco and wanted no filters to stop the flow of the drug. I retrieved my handkerchief and put the butt of Minnow's cigarette inside my pocket. The police missed it. I'll lay it on my desk."

"The hand-rolled cigarette could be from some other day and not be important. I checked with Amy about her business. The street sweepers came through regularly and did their specific lot. The landlord was proud of the fact that his leased areas were clean. I called the company and they swept the lot the day before Amy was shot."

"Then there exist the police photos that I was shown today. One photo caught my eye. I didn't reveal anything at all to Mr. Wright."

Randy stopped talking and stared out the window. He still couldn't believe what he had seen. It was surreal. His eyes misted over again. Then he turned back and went to his hidden marker board. He opened his board to reveal a drawing that matched a specific photograph Derek showed him.

Brake walked over to the marker board and stared at the drawing. He touched the chalk as if he could understand it better. He was perplexed. Randy told the group about the million-dollar life insurance policy Minnow took out on Amy. He also told them Amy bled heavily. The blue area on the drawing was bruising on her body.

Brake's eyes misted over. He liked Amy a whole lot. She was nice to him. Amy's friend, Caro, was in shock. The silence in the room was awesome as reality stared them in the face. There was no room for doubt. The gang knew Minnow shot Amy.

The drawing showed Amy's hand, red with blood from her side where the bullet penetrated. Her finger had drawn a counter-clockwise circle shape twice and an upward swoop which was how she started the first character of Minnow's name. The gang saw her write Minnow's name many times on a bar napkin or coaster. They knew Amy's signature. She was one of those people who placed things on napkins. Amy was telling them her killer while dying. It was clear to all of them; she left the gang a message about her assailant.

Brake started to ask for the vote. All the member's hands were already raised. Brake raised his hand and they looked toward Randy. The vote must be all or nothing. Randy stared at the member's raised hands. He looked at the board, only he was seeing the police photograph etched in his memory. It was hard to believe. The blood was heavy at first and dwindled.

167

Randy raised his hand.

Brake told Randy, "I'll get my man to disconnect the police's stationary camera placed on Minnow's house. It will appear connected and operational to them. We'll set up our own camera in a different place rigged to new wiring. The new gear will be placed so that Minnow won't know about it. He won't see it or find it. One of our gang will constantly monitor the device. As soon as Minnow triggers the camera, the gang will capture him, remove him to a hidden location, and await your instructions."

Randy nodded. Brake thought a minute. It was time for him to take over temporarily.

"The required find and capture message will be relayed to all gang member leaders. I'll let every leader know about the information divulged today and the final vote at this meeting. I will alert the gang leaders about when the funeral plans we've arranged are, so they can pay their respects. Sandra and I will consult on the arrangements and discuss with Randy plans for our future joint gang meeting."

Randy nodded his final agreement and signaled Brake that he needed some space. Brake moved to the door with his team following behind. Brake silently closed the office door.

XXXXXX

Brake and the gang members went to the bar. Their own stresses were pulled into the mix. They all lost a friend. Rhonda poured them each a shot and moved to put the bottle away. The silence in the bar was deafening. The gang's usual comradery was stifled by the drawing of a police photograph. Brake raised his hand and waved her to pour again. No one drank until Brake raised his glass, "To Amy." They all assented the salute.

Her best motorcycle friend, Caro, started crying. She remembered the favor she promised Amy if something happened to her. Caro talked with Amy about it only a month earlier. Caro wondered about the request. She would follow through with the secret request.

Sparky's Bakery would make exactly what was ordered. The order would be made, promptly delivered, and sealed with heavy duty plastic wrap to retain freshness for specialty items.

Caro saluted Amy with the others. She couldn't believe her friend was gone. She missed her friend and would be sad for a long time.

Rhonda would try to help console her about the loss. Rhonda was the queen of loss. She thought this way for a long time. She knew what was required and would take steps to help the girl find new beginnings. She would talk to Caro and teach her how to concentrate on Caro-baby, big time. Rhonda would hurry the process for Caro. There was no time to delay in correcting her mistake and infiltrating more into Randy's business. Caro was her ticket to Brake. Rhonda was sure. She would use everything at her disposal to get Brake to notice Caro. Brake would see a new woman biker appear or else Rhonda wasn't good at her job. Rhonda knew she was way better than good. She was exceptional. Rhonda was on the good side.

38   The Funeral

RANDY READ ALL the cards at the funeral home to keep his mind off the closed white casket. He was surprised to see Skid's bouquet and the realtor man's bouquet of flowers. Randy talked with Amy's realtor friend for some time regarding downtown commercial real estate and immediately liked the man.

He was numb and sat next to Sandra throughout the ceremony she helped arrange. They closed the nightclub to customers and the caterers arrived to handle the outside hamburger barbeque and kegs of beer. Amy loved to eat them constantly. Randy's eyes returned to her casket which was covered in a massive spray of white daisies.

He saw Derek's car later at the cemetery. He wasn't sure if he was paying his respects or hoping Minnow would appear. Randy knew the funeral home and cemetery were the last place the rat would appear. Sandra would return to one of their restaurant locations in the limousine for the regular funeral party. The guests would be given the location before the service. She would handle those guests.

Randy's motorcycle was driven to the cemetery by another member of his party. He saw his motorcycle at the rear of the other motorcycles. Randy nodded to Brake. Brake gave him the sign that everything was ready at the nightclub private party. Everyone left the cemetery except the burial crew. The motorcycle gang headed out to the freeway.

Derek turned to Jim, "Did you notice the large engine motorcycle in the front of the gravesite?"

"Yes, it was a beauty and fit for a king."

"Or a leader of a gang."

Derek turned his car up the ramp to turn around. Looking down the highway, they saw the motorcyclists on the freeway break to single file and the single rider with the large engine move to the front of the line. Derek knew it was Randy on the motorcycle. He switched his suit coat for his leather bomber jacket.

"Randy is now leader of Minnow's gang. Brake was just an interim person. The gang party is at the nightclub. Rhonda and the police are at the wrong reception. Are you up for a short appearance?"

"Yes, if it isn't too close. I don't feel like suicide today." Jim wasn't happy about the change of venue. The two were on their own.

Randy arrived at his nightclub and walked up the outside stairs to the huge deck where the main gang leaders were gathered. He stopped and took note of the hundred or so motorcycles in his parking lot with bikers drinking from paper cups. They all came to salute Amy. He was pleased. Brake motioned to the caterer to begin serving.

Brake came up to Randy and whispered in his ear. Randy turned and located Derek's car on his road in the distance.

"So now you see that I'm the leader of the gang." He watched as Derek's car made a tight turn and left.

Jim looked at Derek, "More trouble."

"I don't think so. I'm almost certain Randy runs a clean shop from all our reports. We might be in luck if the illegal factions break off and some of the other groups move to the legal side. Also, it will add to the numbers of people hunting for Minnow."

"What do you believe the gang will do to Minnow if they find him?"

Derek seriously had given the idea some thought. "I'm not sure, but now Randy, as leader, will have high influence. We need to order a police tail on Randy."

"Perhaps this will be a lucky break and turning point for the police."

Derek certainly needed something more to start working. Jess was on the trip home to San Diego on their yacht. He didn't want her caught in the foray of bad guys. It was an inappropriate time with her being pregnant. He would move heaven and earth to keep her safe. He would be glad when his police detail ended.

The police tail would arrive too late, simply because Randy left earlier. The watchful police van's arrival parked down the street from his home would not escape Randy's wife and her super keen eyes. Sandra would notice the van and smile. She would tell Randy the next time he called about the van. But only after he was safe.

39   Randy Leaving

SANDRA WATCHED AS Randy rolled his clothes like he was in the Army. He attached his side saddlebags to his motorcycle, placing a huge loaded gun in one of the cases with all his permits to carry. Then he securely locked the hard case.

"I don't want you to leave. I don't understand why you must try to find Minnow. Don't you care about me? I hate it when you disappear."

Randy looked at his wife. "Don't even go there. You are the one person who knows how much I love you. I did mean forever. I fell in love with you immediately in the library at the college a long time ago. You're the best thing to enter my life after a small journey away from my hemisphere."

She knew he was talking about her ex-husband. At the time, it was a huge mistake to have gone down that road.

Randy didn't want her to spend another minute thinking about the other man. He knew to talk to her gently.

"Your expertise at marketing and interior design for my restaurants is exceptional. Then there is your teaching the hostesses how to be polite and market the restaurant which blows me away. I need space and time to think. I'm the leader and it is required that I take control of the situation. This ride is for the gang and is personal as well. It is necessary to do this for both of us and our friendship toward Amy. I won't pass the task to anyone else, nor would you."

"I've hated Minnow ever since he asked me out. The Mariana Trench is too shallow a place to park him. He needs to sink deeper into the solid inner core of the hot fiery earth. Yes, I've always supported Amy and especially after seeing how hard she worked at her shop. You're right."

"I will try to put Minnow close to the trench the next time I see him."

"What time are you leaving in the morning?"

"Bright and early, like five o'clock, before the freeway traffic in Los Angeles gets too busy."

Randy took a shower the next morning and fifteen minutes before he was ready to leave, Brake showed up in Randy's driveway with his favorite pillow in green camouflage strapped to his motorcycle chrome backrest bars.

He walked into the house with a bunch of donuts from Sparky's Bakery. Sparky was an older motorcycle friend who let Brake pick up the warm gooey donuts before the store opened. Randy smelled cinnamon and looked at his wife who smiled. Randy loved cinnamon.

"You need a security guard on your trip. Besides, everyone knows it always takes two people to catch a rat. Can I eat some of these rolls now? Sandra told me that I had to wait until I arrived."

Randy kissed Sandra. She slowly let go of his hand.

"Try to come back in one piece."

"I will try because you like my very fit body exactly the way it currently looks."

Randy kissed her one more time. It was good to see her care about his well-being. He didn't want to leave her but knew she would be fine. She did carry her gun in the trunk of the car sometimes, but then she moved it elsewhere. Randy never knew where she parked her gun. He knew not to ask.

Walking into his garage, he handed Brake a special helmet. They could communicate with each other.

"Nice, high-tech helmet with a raven-tinted shield. There are strange buttons. Maybe I shouldn't push them yet. It could be a possible lift off."

Brake placed the helmet on his head. "Hello, is anyone home? There is no answer. Nobody is home. We are going in style on this trip, but my helmet is broken. Maybe you can get your money back."

Randy couldn't refrain from a smile. It would be distraction having Brake along and take longer to research each stop, but it would be more like old times.

"The helmet is working fine. Trust me, it's brand new and not broken. I bought the extended warranty plan. I'll explain how to use the buttons later."

Brake frowned at Randy. He didn't like to wait. He wished that he had done some research on the new helmets. It was one of those things he'd put off.

"Extended warranty for just the parts or the whole helmet? I'm just asking in case I drop it. It's large and hard to hold two bottles at the same time. Usually the bottles win."

Randy sighed. It was too early in the morning. "One more thing you need to remember. No rolled hay stacks."

"Yes, sir. I know the helmet works or you wouldn't have bought it and no more hay stacks."

"Where is my intelligent wife?" She could have explained the advantages and disadvantages of the new helmet design. She had encouraged Randy to purchase them. He glanced at his old helmet on the work bench.

Brake could hardly wait to show him the new green camouflage pajamas he found. He also picked up some gear at the old store that sold used Army stuff. That's why he called one of the gang to put his side saddlebags on his motorcycle.

Randy decided not to show Brake the music button until their first break which would have to be an early lunch. Sandra gave Brake two extra donuts and they disappeared inside Brake's mouth when they hit the edge of Los Angeles.

All Randy could think about were all the places Minnow frequented early in his younger days in southern California. He mapped out the locations on his notebook computer stored in his side case along with a bottle of whiskey.

Randy touched his gold cross that he always carried when he was on the bike. He was going to put it in Amy's coffin, but didn't at the last minute. Amy would want him to carry it on this ride. He wanted to believe life was important and things would work out all right. He was quiet all morning, contemplating the past. After lunch, there would be time for Brake's nonsensical questions.

40   Fixing Up Caro

CARO WALKED INTO the nightclub and asked Rhonda for a cola. Rhonda knew the sad look on a friend's face.

"What is wrong Caro?"

"I miss Brake and Randy."

Rhonda wiped the bar, "Yes, both men are out of the nightclub today. The other bartender gave me the message that neither one will be around this evening. Therefore, I will need to close."

"No, it will be much longer. They are trying to find Minnow."

Rhonda remembered an idea she had about Caro. There was plenty of time with the men out of the way. Perhaps their absence was something she could use to advantage. "Do you like Brake?"

"Plenty of time for what? Yes, I like Brake, but he never pays any attention to me."

Rhonda looked at Caro's dull braided dishwater hair, blue jeans pants and jacket with gray man's t-shirt, and ugly biker boots. There was no makeup and out-of-date pale, blue glasses. She knew exactly what Caro needed.

"Let's have a girl lunch and do some serious shopping. There are some new jeans waiting for us. I'm thinking black, red, turquoise, and possibly green. Some sparkle like lace and rhinestones are required. Perhaps a new hairdo, and we need boots with zippers with swingy fringe. I can get you some Wade Brookston t-shirts for free. You should take this time to concentrate on Caro--baby. You, as a main attraction, will be more dangerous than an all-night keg beer party. Oh, yes, then the men will sit up and notice the new femme fatale. It will be fun."

Caro's mouth opened and shut.

"I love Wade's new album and keep the songs on my new cell phone. I bought the case with rhinestones the other day. Can the hairdresser put some highlights and a little red in my hair? I always wanted to ask Amy for help, but now she is gone. I do want the fringe boots. When can we leave? I'm ready for a new person. Maybe a powerful seductress called Caro--baby, would work. Do you think it could work on Brake?"

"Give me five. We'll make it work."

The two women did a high five with their hands and set the luncheon for the next day, because Rhonda was leaving in a couple days for her vacation. It was the only time Rhonda liked the number five.

Rhonda made appointments for Caro with an optometrist for contact lenses, a makeup consultant, specialty women's shop for new dresses and platform heels, and her jeweler for new diamond stud earrings. The shops would give Caro the discount offered to Rhonda on all products and services.

A red dress and white sheer dress were purchased in case someone asked Caro to Las Vegas. Caro practiced at home walking in her platform heels and increased the hours wearing contacts. She bought new black frames with rhinestones for day use when the contacts were out and red rimmed aviator sunglasses to put on while riding.

When Rhonda returned from her weekend off, she wouldn't recognize the gorgeous woman at the bar talking to two male customers. Her long hair was shoulder length and held in back by a metal flower barrette. The clothes showed her pretty figure. She could hardly wait for Randy and Brake to return and see the wonderful transformation.

Rhonda told Caro she loved the smoky-eye makeup, peach lipstick, and needed to get some of each.

The two women hugged and were now friends. Caro was pleased.

Business in the nightclub picked up when the bikers could see two pretty and happy women behind the bar. The girls worked it and threw bottles of beer across to each other to add to the show. A little foam danced out of the bottles, but the customers didn't care. Tips increased.

41   Rhonda's Yacht Weekend

DEREK AND RHONDA flew from Los Angeles to meet with the yacht at its stopover in Cancun, Mexico. Skid picked them up at the airport and Derek flew them back to the yacht on the helicopter. Rhonda figured it was all right to take her weekend off.

Randy was away for a while and a new manager arrived to take his place while he was out of the office from the nightclub. He also did the close in the evening of the registers at the nightclub.

She stored her luggage in the guest bedroom. Skid smiled and quickly kissed her before going topside. He told her to change into her swimsuit. They were taking the ski watercrafts off the rear of the yacht and inflate the special water dock. It was a perfect day to run the machines close to the shore alongside the beach. He reminded her to splash sunscreen on her body as it was a stunning blue-sky day and the coast was an even better hue of color.

Later the launch took them into the pier to traverse the nightclubs around the hotel district the first evening. He was amazed how wonderful a dancer Rhonda was in the dimly-lit nightclubs. She told him she took lessons for a movie. He wanted to know which movie and Rhonda wouldn't tell him. So, he knew there was some mystery with Rhonda he needed to research. She laughed because he would check with Derek.

Skid bought her wine and dinner with chefs preparing Japanese cuisine at their table on small iron grills. They ate steak, shrimp, and fried rice with no onion. Skid informed her the meal cooking style was called teppanyaki. They dipped the meat and fish in various sauces and selected their favorites.

The next day, they went parasailing, towed behind a powerboat. She loved it but missed the control of the sail. Skid told her he would have to take her paragliding when they were in San Diego. Rhonda could hardly wait. Then she would have to take him skydiving.

"Did you see the woman on the beach with the high-powered cameras taking pictures of us parasailing?"

"You also saw the woman on the beach. I wasn't sure if she was a freelance photographer selling her photos to magazines and websites or someone else. On the ground, I took close-up photos of the woman on my cell phone," said Rhonda.

"Smart move. Can I see the photos? I don't know the woman."

Rhonda shook her head. She also didn't know the woman.

In the evenings after popcorn and movies with the Wrights and Maggie, Skid snuck into her room and stayed until morning.

"The live-with-you forever was looking good. Now that we've become more intimate friends, I can see the picture in my mind."

"I love your skin. What is your nationality?" Skid leaned over and snuck a quick kiss.

"I'm a little French, Swiss, African, and British mainly."

"What is your nationality?"

"Blonde surfer dude with sexy Scandinavian eyes. I don't really know, but my profile certainly fits. I was born in New York City, however, that place makes no sense to me. I've never lived there that I can remember. Maybe my parents moved and didn't tell me. You said intimate. That's an old-fashioned word that hasn't been on my horizon for some time. Can you say it again?"

Rhonda laughed. "I never met anyone like you. You twist your words to make me laugh."

"You mean that in a good way, right?"

"Yes, in an extremely good way."

Now Skid was the one walking on air due to their relationship of mutual high attraction. He knew there was no doubt; he was in love again with a wildly beating heart. He knew Rhonda was coming around to his way of thinking.

"I think that I saw the woman once in Dakar, Senegal, Africa with the divers that left the Wright's motorboat. It is the same camera and it looked like she was asking them questions, but the divers walked away from her," mentioned Rhonda.

"That doesn't sound right. I want you to send the photos of the woman to Derek immediately. I'll talk to him and check with the other divers. The coincidence of seeing this woman again is too much."

"I will do it right away. The last thing we need right now is an unknown tracker on our tails."

Skid returned Derek and Rhonda to the airport on Monday. Rhonda would fly back to Los Angeles and return to work. Derek would fly to Miami.

Derek would call his contacts in Dakar about the strange woman. He also notified his superiors and talked with Jess. Once more information was known about the tracker, he would disseminate to his crony teams and Jim Michaels. He would also check with Ara Jones who lived in Africa some time ago if she knew the strange woman tracker.

Derek and Rhonda needed this break to get refreshed from the recent events.

Derek's mind kept going back to his wife. He was worried about Jess and told his captain to speed up their return schedule. His wife was getting uncomfortable in her pregnancy. He would have to bring in the cronies to protect Jess, the children, and yacht. They both wanted their twin girls born in California, because she told him the two girl's names she selected. He wanted his wife's wish to come true.

42   Domingo Deal

DEREK FLEW TO Miami to meet with the police about a development with Domingo. Matin Domingo wanted to do a deal. His lawyer drafted the proposal which was presented to the various agencies.

The proposal was that Domingo would disclose his African contacts who were the existing game players in the drug, gun, and ammunition's smuggling world for a drop in all charges from that country and those charges from our customs agency.

Next, he would reveal a hit man's name who was currently looking for Minnow Surf. This person could probably find him for the police. Domingo heard about the woman, Amy's murder, and he knew his information would greatly benefit the police in their investigation. The hit man could reveal the woman's name who hired him.

For this impressive information, he required a reduction in his charges in America and wanted to choose a specific prison to spend the rest of his years. The reason for this request was that some of the other prisons held his enemies. There were two last requests. He hated the bed sheets. He wanted different sheets and needed them professionally laundered. He was allergic to the soap the prison used. It gave him hives. He could get them his private doctor's report regarding his allergy. He required fresh fruit and vegetables, not canned.

His lawyer mentioned one more thing. "Domingo wants his snake ring to wear for even an hour during the day. It is now his only treasure. Without it, he becomes ill per his doctor."

Derek shook his head reading the report. There was a picture of the snake ring. The prison Domingo chose was a new, state-of-the-art prison geared toward reform. The photos of the place made it appear like a deluxe hotel compared to the other prisons. There was an extensive library and exercise gym at the prison.

Per the Miami police, the African country would absolve all their charges to capture the main criminals in their country who caused them financial loss for years and years. Our customs people would not drop their charges but could offer a reduction in sentence once they had the information.

The selected prison would also be offered if the information was viable on the hit on Minnow Surf. His special health needs would be verified and worked through to everyone's satisfaction. All the agencies agreed, and the deal was completed with Domingo.

Domingo smiled because he was successful at getting this recent negotiation completed. He met again with his lawyer. The lawyer would start formulating the next deal for Domingo. He told the lawyer the next deal was more extensive, and he wanted a major reduction in his crimes for the information.

Domingo gave his lawyer the account number and codes to an offshore account, so he could get paid for his services. The other account funds were used by the lawyer in processing the first complicated deal and the Miami hit crew.

The confidential information was regarding a woman he dated a long time ago by the name of Shannen Drake. The police knew her by the name, *Snake Woman*. She was an international hired killer whose illusive nature made catching her impossible.

Domingo knew where she lived occasionally when she was in-between jobs. It was a private island. He also knew where she stored her airplanes and helicopters. The last piece of information involved the location of her poisonous snake lab. He felt she hadn't moved the location because the jungle kept it hidden. When he knew her, she died her hair pitch black. She looked like a young Cleopatra.

Remembering his three months together with her when he was a much younger and a more virulent man, he smiled.

"The evil within the woman is controlled at all times."

Shannen was the absolute expert killing machine using silence to her advantage. Her skills at controlling and administering the snake poison shone thanks to the high number of graduate PhD's she possessed.

Domingo told her one time his motto was, "Kill anyone with knowledge which can be used to bring you down, especially if you are unsure about their loyalty."

Domingo and his lawyer were happy with their plan for the next deal with the police. The lawyer left to prepare all the legal papers. He told Domingo this plan would take some extra time. He needed to sit back and relax.

The hit man whose name Domingo gave to the police in his first deal was arrested in Los Angeles. Derek would return to talk to him. The police hoped the information would help locate Minnow Surf and the person who possibly did an illegal act of hiring a murderer.

43 Randy and Brake's Search

RANDY AND BRAKE checked half of the places on the map. Many were more rundown and in seedier neighborhoods than they remembered. Some of the places were gone and a new three-story parking garage existed in one place and took up an entire block.

When Brake put on his green camo pajamas at night, Randy wished he was home with Sandra looking at her body in a silk negligee. He didn't care to see green anything again. He did, however, feel better after the drink and aspirin he allowed himself.

They used some of the Army gear in Brake's saddlebag on a few bad motorcycle people in a nighttime bar called The Hog Kill. The bad guys wanted to fight so Randy and Brake exited in a hurry. Randy had asked Brake before they entered the bar if he was ready. Brake looked at Randy and said, "There's one bike that has a three-foot braided leather cord hanging from his right side. That means he is a leader of the local zone. The cord is to ward off potential nerfs searching this zone."

"Is there any use to the leather cord other than to strangle someone?"

"Of course, a cord can also lead to entrapment."

Randy looked at Brake. "Seriously?"

"Yup."

"Then I grant you all the power to use whatever you know to move forward."

Brake smiled. He bent a few sprinklers and lighted his old cigar that was half burnt and six years old that he pulled from his biker bag. Randy shook his head. He had no clue where Brake found things. Randy leaned back and let the scenery roll. Brake was his bodyguard and he knew things would be well shortly. Brake was a crazy-good person to have on board. Randy sent a prayer thanking his wife.

The bad bikers chased after them. One of them was smoking an old stogie like Brake. Brake pulled alongside the man and blew his staled cigar smoke in his direction. The man smelled the stink and chased after Brake. Brake was delighted that the man fell for his trap. Brake weaved in and out playing the chase man with his motorcycle. Brake waited for the right moment. "It was destruct time."

Brake looked at Randy for his approval and saw Randy was cruising. Then Randy looked over and gave Brake the *okay-nod*. It was the perfect moment. Brake took the second biker position, while Randy took the lead. It was their fallback plan to lure the angry biker men closer. They would speed up to chase which was namely Randy, ignoring Brake's movements. Brake would position his bike to grab their lead biker. Brake threw out his recent find at a pawn shop, the army net. It was camo-colored and strong. The net had been hardly used at all. The army net caught in the first one's wheels and pulled him into the ditch. The long knife he was carrying bounced on the pavement and hit the second biker in the right leg, stopping him fast.

For the third biker, Brake pulled out a couple of fake grenades that held an entire string of firecrackers. Still smoking an inch of the evil cigar which had to be burning hot, Brake somehow lit a sparkler while steering the bike. The fuses ignited. Releasing the first grenade in a backward arc, it bounced high in the air, firing away over the biker. Brake was surprised that the sound or smoke hadn't scared the third biker off.

The third biker was still approaching. Randy looked at Brake and shrugged confusion. Brake wasn't about to quit. He had more toys stored in the bag. Brake reached for the super sparkle, loud, fiery, black-fire smoke bombs with rockets. They were only a year old and were kept hidden in a secret compartment on the bike. Brake flipped the lid and pulled out his hidden treasure. Brake pulled out his treasure and waved the items to Randy who was riding super close. Randy grinned and pressed his foot to the accelerator to remove himself from the location of firepower. It was show time.

Brake slowed until his bike was alongside the third obstinate bad guy. He tossed the second lit round in the biker's lap. The bundle stuck on the guy's jacket and wrapped around his belt buckle. The paper was unfolding from the bottle rockets around the buckle as the wind whirled around the bike. Brake lit his lighter, wrapped sparklers with electrical tape, ripped off the tape, and let the bundle land in the biker's lap to light the whole bundle of firepower. Suddenly, the ignition fused, the bundle lit, fireworks lifted, and smoke filled the air. There was no way a biker could drive through the mess. Brake and Randy saw the third biker spinout and kickstand the bike. He ran and dove into the ditch that was filled with six inches of water from a recent rain. Finally, the biker must have believed the better of his enemies. He was seen running from the scene. Brake and Randy heaved a sigh of relief. The Hog Kill group were brought down, at least temporarily. In the future, Randy would accidentally turn over the bad group's name to the police. It was payback. Randy bought his friend new exotic cigars and a better grade of sparklers. A large box appeared one day with an entire pig skin.

Brake looked around after leaving the third biker. There was no one to see him litter the highway. He threw away the half-burnt sparkler, the wire bounced to the side of the road where the last biker had stopped. The red-hot glowing sparkler hit the windshield and burned a crease across the front rubber.

Brake caught up with Randy and they drove in sync for another one hundred miles. Both men knew they shouldn't drive through that small town ever again. Otherwise, they would need more than fireworks. They would need an entire army. They sent the message across to their bikers to stay away.

Randy told Brake, "We did push things a little too far with the local gang of thugs and thieves. One of the bad bikers must not have liked your rebel flag. You should find a different flag."

Brake showed him the two open fresh bottles of beer he was holding that he grabbed off their table. Randy hadn't yet paid for them. He then wondered how

Brake held the beers and lit the sparkler at the same time. He suddenly didn't want to know. Brake let go of his flag. He had had enough.

They both laughed and chugged the cold bottles of beer. Randy and Brake started to feel better about the whole ride.

"Just like old times. But I think I'm getting too old for this type of action." Randy exited his bike.

"I'm positive there is no action or movement on my bottom side. It's numb. Do you think they have seats a little wider in the back for my bike?"

Randy couldn't help, but smile. He tried to visualize the seat cushion.

"Maybe you should design one. You still have the special software on your computer that Caro gave you last year. It was a smart move. She knew that you took that computer class and was excited. She believes that you can do amazing things. I think that you might have a gift with her help. Speaking of Caro's level-headed smarts in the computer world, why haven't you ever asked Caro out on a date? It is clear to the gang that she likes you best. And we all like Caro."

Brake told him, "I'm afraid of women. Don't tell anyone. Yes, I'll try the software when we return home. I have to read the manual first."

That made Randy laugh even more. It was time to enlighten Brake.

"I won't tell. Caro could help teach you. She talked with me at length about the software. That would be better than a manual. Hands-on training with a guru sounds like perfect education. You need to understand some things. Women can be as gentle as a lamb or as crazy as a lioness. A smart woman is hard to find."

Their discussion made Brake sit up taller. He forgot about the software. There was one thing that he knew about her. Caro went to cat shows in the area on weekends. He could go with her to a safe cat show. Then he remembered that he knew nothing about cats. He heard they liked noisy feather toys on a wand. The judge wouldn't mind if he held his toy at the special ring, too. Or was that the game they called, Cat Out? He would have to think about the comparison of a lamb and lioness. Perhaps he could buy Caro a kitty. It should be gentle and quiet as a lamb. His friend owned a cat they called Aby that was asleep when Brake visited. He couldn't remember the name, but it was like the liquor called absinthe. Brake snapped his fingers. He recalled the name of the cat species.

"Abyssinian is the cat's breed name."

Randy wondered how Brake's brain moved to pedigreed cats.

Brake wasn't sure why his friend installed a cable holding the cat tower to the wall. It probably was the cat's exercise gym and the creature liked to walk the tightrope. He knew a person who made real sturdy cat towers and probably could include the mechanism in the design. Brake would call his friend when he returned home.

XXXXXX

195

The next day, they decided to check another pawn shop. Randy showed Minnow's picture to the owner. He couldn't recall the person, but then he couldn't recall his friend's faces either. It was probably those bad glasses he's worn for the last twenty-five years.

Brake pointed to the glass case at a gold ring with a design that looked like a pond. The owner retrieved the ring. Randy nodded his head.

"It is Minnow Surf's ring. The ring is the one that creepy friend of his wore. You remember the guy with green eyes. He gave me the chills with his talk of chemicals. Minnow must need money if he left the ring in the shop. He was somehow proud of owning the object. That means he may be moving back to his original rat hole."

Randy knew it was time to return home.

"I will call our people and let them know to raise the alert."

"Thanks, Brake, I appreciate it."

Brake found a pirate biker flag in the pawnshop. Three circles of white were on the flag in a corner which probably was from bleach spill. Brake looked at the spots and was reminded of a ghost. He could put temporary black marker ink over the spots. No one would know the spots were on the flag except him. It could be his beer magic trick, because beer always removed the ink. He would install the flag on the motorcycle later. Brake bought another faded rebel flag. The rebel flag would look good in his bathroom at home.

Randy and Brake left the pawnshop knowing where Minnow might be hanging out.

44   Interview with Hit Man

THE POLICE WERE unable to retrieve information from a hit man hired to find Minnow. They asked Derek to talk with the man. The police were used to Derek's negotiation techniques. His high ability to figure out a con artist and beat him at the game were excellent skills to own.

Derek entered the room and sat down with his folder.

"The name on my report shows that you are Jake Kendro from Los Angeles. Is that correct?"

The man grunted.

"My name is Derek Wright and the police brought me into their little soiree to resolve some issues."

"First, there is a really known criminal by the bad dude name of Matin Domingo from Miami who is a peregrine falcon fan. He even considers himself the true falcon who has wisdom about things within his turf and elsewhere. He sees all and knows all. But as it turns out, that maybe was just a ruse or cliché in the police-turf side of things. So, there is still the criminal-turf left wide open. But, alas, we will tell you the police side of the story. Domingo did get caught just like you did. Domingo is in prison, a cushy one, for stealing drugs, guns, and miscellaneous other things."

"Secondly, somehow this supreme falcon and his kingdom, who eat people for lunch, know about your hit business. Domingo is using this information to do an exchange with the police in Miami for a request of his own. Domingo traded your name to them. Are you clear on the story so far?"

Again, another grunt.

"Third one is the shocker. If the police receive no information from you, the favor marker expires. The police walk away. You will be left alone standing next to an extremely hungry, two-hundred-mile-per-hour, diving, peregrine falcon and his team. Domingo's team always catch their prey. End of story. You can have ten minutes to make your decision."

Derek got up and left the folder on the table. The man looked at the photo of a falcon eating its prey. Then he looked at a picture of Matin Domingo. They both looked hungry. The sweat started rolling off the man named Jake.

Derek took a coffee break. Usually ten minutes did the trick. He kept his skills finely tuned.

When he returned, Derek remained standing. The man named Jake started talking to Derek.

"I was hired by a woman who disguised herself. We met at a coffee shop in Santa Monica that I know contains no cameras. The woman did give me a picture of the candidate for removal with his name and address. She drove a hard bargain with me and would only give me twenty-five-thousand-dollars total for the hit, one-quarter of the amount was provided immediately. The rest of the money she would hold until the candidate was removed from the area. She didn't care about the method of removal."

"So, she never actually stated the words kill or murder? She only mentioned removal from the area. Did she give you a name?"

"Yes, to both questions."

"What was her disguise?"

"She wore old clothes, bad shoes, great makeup, and a gray wig. But her nails were recently manicured with bright red nail polish like she was high society. There was her ring which didn't go with her costume. It had gold and diamonds in a flower shape. It looked like a one of a kind ring or an older design."

"Do you know where Minnow currently is located?"

"No, I don't. I tracked the man south and then lost him at a pawn shop. The man at the pawn shop said the man became ill and had some medicine pen which he used outside the shop."

"Do you remember the name of the pawn shop?"

"It's this shop on the corner, Street's Pawn Place, in Encinitas, California."

"Thanks for the information. The police will check out the place you did mention. If you remember any insight about the woman, you should disclose it to the police."

Jake grunted. Then his eyes lit up. "Her name was Chandra. Maybe it was Mandra or Candra. There, I did help the police. I gave them what they wanted so I should be safe, right?"

Derek's eyes darkened, and he developed a strange look on his face as recognition dawned. Jess told him the impossible was truly possible. He wondered if the woman's husband knew about the purchased hit. He would request a meeting with the woman and her lawyer.

"The police can fill you in on the rest of your arrest."

Derek left the police building to round Jim from his nap. He wanted him to reach the pawn shop before closing. They needed all the details from the owner of the shop. Jim would get back with Derek.

45   Possible Chandra Person

DEREK'S SECRETARY INFORMED him the lawyer arrived with his client and they were waiting for the woman's husband who was on his way. Derek smiled at his secretary and told her to offer the lawyer and the woman coffee. Derek formulated the questions for the meeting in his mind. He would need to proceed cautiously.

The lawyer, Sandra, and Randy Moore walked into Derek's office. Derek noticed Randy's full beard, red eyes, and motorcycle clothes. He knew he drove at night to arrive at this meeting. Sandra wore no rings on her hands but did wear red fingernail polish. She looked well put together as did their lawyer. Introductions were made.

The Moore's lawyer demanded, "What is the reason for the meeting? I'm only told that it involves a hit upon Minnow Surf. That man is not my client."

Randy looked at their lawyer and back to Derek. He wouldn't look at Sandra and she knew exactly why he was upset with her. Sandra knew to remain calm and never answer a question directly. Her knowledge of how to distract men was huge. She would have made an excellent stage actress. Sandra went into loving wife mode which always worked.

Derek knew Sandra talked with Randy. He would have liked to listen to their conversation. It would have started with something like the words nuts or crazy. Derek suddenly felt sorry for Randy, because he surely was in the same spot with Jess in Napa, California, a long time ago.

It was about women with secrets. He reminded himself his intent of this meeting was to see if they knew anything about Minnow and to possibly rattle Randy's cage.

"The police have in custody a hit person who was hired by a woman from Los Angeles who would pay him twenty-five-thousand dollars. The woman only gave our prisoner one-fourth the amount of the fee to remove Minnow Surf from the area. The woman is high society because her red nails were recently manicured, and she wore a one of a kind gold and diamond flower ring. The man thought he could recognize the woman or her voice again. The woman told him her name was Chandra."

Randy looked at the ceiling.

"I brought you to this meeting to ask if you do know anyone by that name or who may own such a ring? Your relationship to Amy might provide the police clues to the person who did hire a known con artist on the street to possibly perform an illegal act. The woman did ask the man for removal, except that is not the same as asking for a kill or murder. But it does show intent."

Derek looked directly at Randy.

The lawyer responded, "My clients do not know such a person who would potentially perform this illegal task. Can my clients now leave or is there a further matter?"

"Yes, do any one of you know Minnow's location?"

"The answer to the question is absolutely not," responded the lawyer as if he rehearsed the line.

"Then you also do not know his last location was Encinitas?"

Randy volunteered, "We did lose the tracks to Minnow there. We were searching for the man also to encourage him to turn himself into the police."

Derek knew he just lost control of the meeting. He must leave them with an important point.

"I bet you are good at poker." Derek looked at Randy.

"But, I would encourage you to get Minnow to do just that, turning himself in. The idea is an excellent one. We don't want anyone to become hurt in the scuffle."

Derek thanked them for coming to his office and ushered the three people to his office door.

He knew there would be a storm at the Moore house this evening by the look on Randy's face right before Derek shut his office door.

46 Randy's Wife Discussion

RANDY FILLED THE motorcycle with gas and called Brake to let him know the police were hot on Minnow's trail and knew about Encinitas. He told him briefly about the meeting with Derek. Brake stayed with his sister and was headed back home to await the rat. Randy told him there was no mention of the police monitor on Minnow's house. He thought that was good news.

Randy walked into his home to an awaiting wife in her designer living room. He sat down and removed his biker boots.

Sandra winced so he took them out to the kitchen, threw them onto the doorway rug, and removed his jacket. He went to the bar and made themselves both a drink. He could tell by her posture she felt she owned every right to her decision. Randy knew he was messed up no matter how he approached his intelligent wife, Sandra. He had missed her.

He looked at his completely-paid designer home, went into the living room, and sat down. Randy slowly sipped his drink letting her take the lead.

"I hate Minnow for constantly creating a mess in our life. I did want him removed."

"I know that you are not fond of the guy, but not too many people like Minnow. However, they don't hire a hit, or I would know about it. You clearly did hire one. Derek knows you ordered that one. So now you

205

make me responsible. I do owe the man called Derek Wright a favor. He will call in the marker."

Sandra crossed her arms.

Randy wanted to be done with the conversation. He was sore and tired.

"You did cross the line like I informed you during our call the previous evening. And that is why we are now having this heated discussion. I'm the leader and I expect you to communicate with me. I also am your husband and am totally blind-sighted by your actions, which by the way, are illegal. The semantics of the word remove are debatable which Derek nicely pointed out to me and our lawyer. I believe even our lawyer was surprised today. You know that I'm not in the removal type of business, currently."

Sandra started to get upset with her husband. He was choosing the wrong side in this conversation. She expected his support. He left her alone hours on end and Minnow was the one out of control.

Randy saw his wife's anger and knew what was coming.

"All I want is your attention. You're always busy and never want to take vacation anymore. I've wanted to go on a cruise and you can't even talk about it. You have this junk going on with the man all the time. I did keep dwelling on these other issues and shouldn't have done so. Everything is a stressful mess in my world. It's even worse in our world." Sandra started crying.

Randy knew he was now in complete trouble with her. Figuring Sandra out was a challenge for him.

He hated women crying. He went over to her and put his arm around his wife.

"Yes, I'm busy, but I will try to be better, and you can plan our cruise. But you must never do this again, because I don't want to visit you in jail. That is why I'm so upset. It isn't about the money, but I thought the final price was too high. Do you understand?"

"I do. You must promise me that you won't be stupid. I don't want to visit you in jail either. The price was a little off." She glanced sheepishly at Randy. She could see he was coming around. Forgiveness was close at hand.

"I will try to be careful."

Randy kissed his wife and asked her to wear something soft, because he couldn't take anymore green camouflage flannel pajamas.

"Was it that bad?"

"Worse."

Sandra kissed her husband. Things would be all right between them. She asked him about the flower ring and thought it should be replaced.

"Yes, you can start looking for a new one."

Sandra kissed her generous and loving husband. She would wear her new nightgown.

Randy went to their master bathroom to shave and take a long hot shower. He could hardly wait to sink into their special and expensive foam mattress with the dual remote controls to raise the head and feet of the bed. He deserved some luxury after the motorcycle trip. In the morning, he would almost feel human again.

47 Shannen's Island

SHANNEN DRAKE LOOKED out her floor to ceiling windows from her opulent one level home. The home sat close to the aqua-blue ocean. She lived on an island property. Seeing her man, Max Lewis, arrive on one of her many float planes, she saw him jump onto the long dock. She would join him in the meeting room.

Max entered the meeting room and asked her which report she wanted to view first.

"Today, I will view the Miami report first."

After reading the report, she raised two fingers indicating both people must be terminated. They were people she released from her company. They were two former trackers who went rogue. Their contract allowed them a certain dollar figure in investigative services outside her company.

Both were cheating her and skimming large amounts of money and gifts from her clients. They only selected a few new clients on their own. The latest gift was a supped-up red sports car with expensive silver rimmed wheel covers that one of her clients bought in Los Angeles. The driver's door looked repainted. She turned to him.

"What do you think of the sports car door?"

"Yes, the sports car door was redone, possibly a chop-shop incomplete which means cops. Do you want the standard method?"

"No, I want you to surprise me. Make it look suicidal. Take your time to make the death look all right and you can hire this one out to a customer in the underworld."

He handed her the second report labeled Los Angeles.

"This strange gang is new and moving into my pricier business."

She took her magnifier and looked at the tattoo. Snake design was also something the former trackers were not allowed to use. She knew the artist and his ink man.

"Let's monitor them a little longer. I need knowledge of all players, locations, and the rest of their business. Contact the artist and warn him with permanent failure. First, I must have name and location of the person who ordered the design. The artist will understand my language and disappear. If they aren't former trackers, then we must reconsider our dealings with an unknown entity."

Max reluctantly handed her the third folder. His snake diamond ring shown in the light.

She was pleased he had it polished and the diamond eyes shown. It was the same design as the ring she gave her friend in Miami. She smiled remembering Matin.

She saw Max's hesitation. She held her hand out for the report. Shannen read the report about Matin Domingo's arrest and imprisonment. She waved Max the signal their meeting was completed.

Max believed she needed time to make her decision about her former lover. He was correct.

The *Snake Woman* had much to contemplate. It was a long time since she saw Matin. His illegal activities never crossed into her business. Yet, he knew too much about her and her empire. She wondered if he would use the knowledge as a bargaining chip to save himself.

Knowing the answer to her question, she needed to be sure. She called her top tracker to retrieve information from Domingo's lawyer and gain it secretly. Shannen couldn't order the kill now. Memories of their time together were interfering with her judgment.

She crossed over to the bar and downed three shots of her favorite Russian vodka. The beauty of the day was lost to her. The amazingly strong liquor from her mother's homeland was addictive. Her name came from her Irish father who raised her in Ireland and sent her to the prestigious universities in Europe. Traveling extensively with her father, she became accomplished in many languages.

She met Max one time on her many vacations to Hong Kong. Shannen spent vacations in the summer as a child visiting her mother in Russia. When her mother died, she tried to close the old rambling estate. But decided she needed the roots. Leaving her parent's caretaker couple in charge of the property, they maintained the house and buildings. The surrounding land was leased to a quiet farmer for growing a fast summer wheat crop.

The estate was transferred to a corporation that she owned through another couple entities.

Over the years, she built a special building on the estate with a tunnel to the house. Installing hydroponic growing systems for vegetables and fruit, she also brought in egg-laying chickens. Between the animals on the property and the garden system, a person could sustain themselves sufficiently, without needing anything from the outside. Only an occasional run to town was required for dry goods. Generators were installed in case of power failure.

She exchanged out the small engines in the old identical trucks with large diesels. Her own larger gas tanks were installed. Snowmobile machines were purchased for their hunting of caribou. There was a tiny lake on the property which was great to run the machines around the edge.

Installing security fences and gates around the property, she included a technically-sound security room inside the house with cameras viewing strategic locations. Computer equipment and heavy-duty weaponry were in every room in the house hidden behind mirrors. An exercise room and new library were completed.

Secret passageways were in the house built a long time ago by her family. The inside of the home was grandeur and elegance. The dishes and linens were bought from stores in Dublin. Shannen was responsible for the change. She bought winter clothing and boots for herself and Max. Included were a few fur coats. Shannen went into town on occasion with the caretakers so people in the small village would be familiar with her face and natural strawberry blond hair. There were no cameras in any of the stores to take her picture. They didn't bother her when she told them she was recently widowed and was renovating the old farm she purchased to live there permanently, someday.

In the meantime, she was stressing out. Shannen tried to calm down. Her normal solid control was slipping. Her old friend was in jail and she worried. If the police became involved in a deal with Matin, she would need to make quick decisions. Shannen knew her island home could possibly be gone. No one around her would see the turmoil except Max who steadied her several times. He worried about his own future and knew he had nowhere to go. She was his life. If she went down, he would be beside her. His loyalty was very strong.

While Shannen waited, she visited her snake compound. It was her favorite place. There was always new research completed for her review. Some of her older snakes were failing, and she gave the compound leader the order to put them down. They serviced her well for past hits against her enemies.

48   First Restaurant Gone

MINNOW CHECKED THE blowing package and clock device. He could never remember how to set the clock. Randy always took care of that piece of equipment. They used to do mini-explosives in their search in the hills for gold when they were in their teens. They found a tiny piece of gold and thought they would find riches until this old man kicked them off his property. Minnow guessed, set the clock, and left the area.

At two o'clock in the morning, the kitchen area blew in Randy's triple-star restaurant. Luckily the security guard was on the outside grounds, away from the kitchen area. The guard called Brake and Randy who arrived on their motorcycles in the parking lot.

Brake waited because Randy moved Sandra to a safe location and called two gang members to protect her.

Randy knew Minnow tried to figure the clock to set it to two o'clock in the afternoon when Sandra would be at the restaurant for her salad lunch. Sandra read in a magazine somewhere that leafy vegetables helped make a person smarter and improved memory function. There was improvement in her figure as well. Sandra was a target for helping Amy at her shop. Sandra told Randy after the funeral about the shoving abuse incident Minnow created at the beauty shop. She told him it was the one time she forgot and left her gun in her purse. She would have liked to use her little pistol. Randy knew that episode was a close call because his wife's aim was accurate. This latest episode with Minnow changed things. The attack on Randy's parachute was overlooked, but Randy would not allow anything more to happen to his family or businesses.

All the gang leaders were informed. The Nevada secondary leader whose group broke off and left Randy's gang found out about the blown restaurant and which person was the suspect. It was hard not to miss the burned area when they drove down the road. They contacted their leader who was in prison over the Nevada drug bust. The Nevada people would also begin looking for Minnow.

The restaurant place was in high flames when the police and fire trucks arrived. Randy and his security guard talked to the police. Randy told them he thought it was arson created by Minnow Surf. The head fireman approached the policeman and showed him a piece of explosive wrapper. It was certainly arson.

XXXXXX

Derek was awakened at his warehouse where he was staying in Los Angeles. His yacht entered United States waters a half hour ago, per his captain. Derek listened to the police phone call and started dressing while still on the device. Derek contacted the yacht captain to change course and let Jess know their new plans. She was used to changes and he knew her acceptance would ease everyone's concerns on the yacht the next morning.

Jess laid awake and could feel the yacht turn directly out to sea. She put her housecoat on and let the captain into their bedroom. He quickly told her about Derek's call and left. Jess sat down on the bed. The small babies were kicking. Her time was close. She was happy they were headed to Catalina Island. The rest of the Wrights also loved to be there. The inflatable dock for the ski watercraft would be brought out and placed on the end of the yacht. There would be hot dogs and brats for lunch, French fries, and ice cream shakes. Extra security was traveling in a smaller boat to meet with their yacht. They also liked watching and playing with the ski watercraft and the Wright children.

Derek arrived at the fire and saw total insurance loss. He talked with Randy who confirmed that he thought Minnow was responsible. Randy explained their past experiences with explosives. Derek knew it was a direct hit aimed at Randy and his wife. The search would ramp even further to find Minnow. He hoped it would be soon. Derek sent out messages to his teams.

Randy closed all his businesses down for a week to install new security at all locations and interviewed extra security people. Then the extra security would be in place upon reopening. He moved Sandra permanently to a new location until Minnow could be caught. Extra security was placed around his home. Randy increased the insurance loss amounts on his home and businesses. There was a high possibility his cousin would try some other means to destroy anything Randy owned.

49   Gang Caught Minnow

IT WAS A RAINY drizzle and gray day when the trigger on Minnow's house went off on the camera the gang installed. The gang members were contacted to move into their places. They watched as Minnow retrieved some bundle under his bed. They figured it was money.

Randy arrived, and the gang silently withdrew their guns and stormed the residence breaking down doors and windows in the process. Minnow knew there was no time to escape as twenty guns were aimed at him with his single revolver. The chamber of the revolver held six bullets, but he felt the bullets roll loosely in his other pocket. He debated for a minute. He saw Brake smile. Minnow figured there wasn't enough bullets to make a stand unless he could get another couple guns. That idea was too much work.

He knew the limousine keys were by the door that led to the porch which connected to the garage. Minnow also saw a basket in the porch from Sparky's Bakery with his favorite homemade crispy bars. There was white frosting on some of them. Those were the best ones. He was hungry.

Leaving his motorcycle keys on the nightstand when he flipped the bed over, Minnow knew he would take the limousine to a dealer close to the airport to get more cash when he made his escape. Minnow hated driving on the super busy Highway 405 because cars moved slowly, but he would risk it.

He planned on escaping because he knew Randy wouldn't kill him right away. Minnow smiled. He slowly lowered his revolver which held no bullets. He forgot to load the chamber. Brake kicked the empty gun out of the way.

The gang backed away and let Randy approach Minnow. Minnow started circling, because the cousins had done this dance before.

"Why, Minnow?"

"Because she was the one who did me wrong. It's her fault, not mine."

"And the bruises you gave her are her fault as well? You aren't a man. There is a word we call you. It is abuser. You shot her because she wanted a new life. You could have let her go. She was a valuable human being and you didn't give her a chance. I'm almost done talking. The gang did vote."

Minnow stopped and looked at the gang. He knew if that was the way it was going to be, he would charge Randy. Randy calculated the space and motion, hitting him in the stomach with a right clip to the face. Minnow dropped down.

"The first hit is for the cut ropes on my parachute."

He hit Minnow a second time in the stomach, very hard, which brought Minnow to his knees.

"That is for Amy."

Randy hit him hard in the face. "That is for Sandra and blowing my favorite restaurant which started a fire. It's my turn to decide if I blow you to kingdom come. Besides, when I set the clock, it will be accurate. I might let you watch the clock."

Randy turned to leave, and Minnow came after him throwing a couple punches. He knocked Randy off balance. Freaking out, Randy pummeled Minnow, and the gang pulled him off. He cooled down and motioned for them to tie him up.

The gang sat a limp, bleeding Minnow in the chair, tied him tightly, and taped his hands and legs. Randy left the house. Brake came over and kicked Minnow in the legs.

"That's for Amy, too. I have binoculars in my bike, and I might want to see the clock hit the sweet number. Kaboom, no more troublemaker, and no more pieces to clean up after. Do you think there'd be any ashes left to bury? Hardly!"

The gang would let Minnow rot a while in his own mess. They wanted him to worry first about his crime and second, what the gang planned for him. They would wait for Randy's final decision. The gang didn't want to wait but were trained to follow their leader.

A guard of two gang members was posted for the night to watch Minnow. The next morning the gang would find Minnow gone and two of their members stabbed. Both would live to tell the tale that Minnow escaped with the limousine.

Randy's gang exited the area searching for the pricey vehicle.

Minnow would lay low for a week, hiding the vehicle in the garage of one of his old chauffeurs, whom he tied up until it was time to leave. The chauffeur's house was well stocked with food and groceries from the market delivery person who arrived in the afternoon. The chauffeur went to the door with a gun at his back and Minnow by his side. He paid the delivery boy. Then the chauffeur was retied up again.

The morning police crew noticed their camera at Minnows house showed dry ground and it was raining. They went to the house and noticed the mess. They let Derek know there was some scuffle and the limousine was missing. They put a report out for the limousine.

Derek surveyed the house and knew Minnow tangled with the gang. He contacted Randy about Minnow's house. Randy told him it was probably teenagers having a party. He still did not know Minnow's location and was looking for him. Derek figured the bad guy was still alive, but he hoped he was a little damaged.

50 Randy's Decision

AFTER FIGHTING WITH Minnow, the rain stopped. The California sky peeked through the disappearing dark clouds. Too many clouds existed for a skydiver jump. Randy made himself breathe in the moist air and reminded himself there was a good life waiting for him besides this current disaster.

Selecting a bouquet from the small florist shop, he chose white daisies with a few pink carnations and green bell flowers thrown into the mix. Randy went to Amy's grave hoping for some enlightenment regarding his choice about Minnow's future. Laying the flowers down, he left the cemetery.

He was entrusted with the final decision. Whatever course he chose, the gang and his wife would support him. They trusted him totally. After leaving the bouquet on the grave, he drove to his home. Walking in his den, he poured himself a drink. Sandra brought him a large ham sandwich and a hot cup of coffee because she knew he would not sleep. She kissed him and left him alone.

Thoughts of the past enveloped him. He saw the mess and destruction surrounding Minnow. Things worsened once he was released from prison and Amy left him. He had seen the madness in Minnow's eyes when they were circling each other. Randy knew the man belonged in a cage.

221

The decision to kill Minnow was a high one on the gang's list. But Randy knew he must consider the legal ramifications and his own conscious. He could rationalize he had every right to kill the man because he declared war on his family. Self-defense could be one avenue. Randy's right to protect his loved ones and businesses could reign supreme. He knew his wife's thoughts about where she would like to see Minnow parked permanently. Minnow tried to kill her with a bomb. A jury would understand the logic of protection.

Then there was the involvement of his wife and gang who could become accessories to murder and spend the rest of their lives in prison. There would be no understanding by a jury other than an exemption for Sandra. Lastly, there was Randy's conscious.

"There is right and wrong. Do I allow the guilt of a murder decision into my life? I have every right in the world to kill. It is an eye for an eye right now. Minnow murdered someone I love. Revenge is there wanting, staring me in the face, and urging me to proceed. Revenge provides powerful escape. Do I give in to revenge? There is open on the table another path. The path was one rarely chosen. Their gang didn't work with the police. There existed the choice to turn him over to the police and let justice decide the fate of Minnow Surf's life. Prison would lock the evilness away from society. Randy knew things in the legal system would move slowly but the man would no longer create trouble for them. This was the route Mr. Wright had encouraged him to take.

Randy looked at the clock and finally crawled in bed with his wife at four o'clock which would give him a few hours' sleep. The crossroad he just encountered was two open lanes of highway, like in the desert, with nothing in sight. There was no one there to influence him on direction. Randy could drive right or left. A bird flew past him.

"The bird represents life. I wonder where there is a tree or water for the bird to live."

He made his decision. It was the direction the bird flew.

Randy knew in his heart the path chosen was the correct one.

51   Close Enough

MINNOW SAW A recorded rock concert on the chauffeur's television set. The heavy metal rocker was Wade Brookston from Miami who would sing and dance with a special young guest at his show. Minnow reached for the television remote to turn the channel. The rocker announced his guest as Justin Wright with the entire Wright entourage in the audience. The camera crew did a sweep of the twenty guests and Minnow saw Jess Wright sitting next to Derek in a long black lace gown. She was holding Derek's arm in anticipation waiting for her son to appear.

Backing the scene up on the television set with the remote, he stopped the frame to view it once more. It occurred to him the Wrights were in Miami.

"Their son could sing well. Of course, they have money for expensive lessons for him to meet rich friends. Justin doesn't need to steal bikes or rob banks. I wouldn't be in this mess if I had his lifestyle."

He walked into the chauffeur's bedroom and stole the old man's identification card and went online. Minnow purchased a ticket with the old man's credit card. He found his toupee in a drawer with a large bobby pin, an old hat, and jacket. Next, he picked up the old man's extra set of glasses and wore them.

Checking the bedroom mirror, he realized that he could pass the security check in.

The next morning, Minnow called the life insurance company. He wanted to know when he would receive his million dollars from his wife's death. The woman told him, 'Technically your divorce finalized three days before the police report which per Section Ten, Paragraph H of your policy, the divorce means the policy is null and void."

There was no sound from Minnow on the phone.

"Sir, are you still on the line," asked the curious insurance worker.

"Yes, but I'm confused."

"Of course, you are. Let me explain. The signed life insurance policy is the first in. The document is the first to arrive as part of your request to our company's special inventory department. We can allocate funds into your inventory slot. The signed and dated signatures on the second set of documents have reset the clock. Don't you love the analogy to a clock? The timing is correct for the insurance company. The clock takes the allocation out of your inventory slot. The money is now back into our company's super-locked vault which makes it available for the next transaction. The concept is like FIFO in accounting.

Minnow couldn't believe it. The woman talked like Sandra with her Mary place.

"I don't care about the Fido dog in accounting. So, do I get my million dollars or not?"

The insurance woman shook her head. This client was the person in the doghouse. She responded, "Nada, zip, or another word is zero."

The insurance woman was out of the office on a sick day when her superiors told every employee this policy was a police matter and any calls must be reported immediately to the supervisor. She also hadn't read her huge quantity of emails.

Minnow was speechless.

He counted on this money to fund his escape to Canada. It was a million dollars gone. Amy tricked him and made him lose a million dollars. Everything was her fault. Then he remembered the Wrights in Miami. They tricked him out of this money somehow. He knew they did. They cost him the million dollars. He had it in his inventory slot. The money should still be there. His anger built higher and higher.

He grabbed four crispy treats from the basket before he left.

XXXXXX

The old chauffeur was forced to drive a very violent man to the airport who kept waving the gun towards him. The old chauffeur stopped looking in the mirror at the madman in his backseat. He kept his eyes on the road. He knew Minnow had flipped over the edge.

The old man could feel his heart jumping all over the place. He looked at the gas mileage and there was barely a quarter tank left. He hoped the gas would be enough to reach their destination. He remembered a sports car race where two of the men were in the lead on the last lap when they ran out of gas. The old man was beginning to know how those race car drivers felt. Then he remembered when he used to sit in the stands and watch the big race. He almost forgot about the bad guy in the limousine.

The old man thought he would be the one hitting his final resting place shortly. The chauffeur knew that he lived too long, and it was his time to crash and burn.

Meanwhile, a gang member spotted the limousine on Highway 405. The limo was heading toward the airport with Minnow inside. Randy's gang assembled their guns and quickly took side roads to catch up with the slow-moving traffic on the 405. They were close to the limousine when it pulled off one of the ramps heading north.

Checking his saddlebag to verify the police handcuffs were inside, Brake felt better. During the week, Brake went through several pawn shops to find something better that Minnow couldn't knife his way out of while in capture mode. The handcuffs were a little rusty, but the key worked to lock the hands tight. It took Brake a long time to get them to reopen with the key. He figured that was why they were in the shop. Brake didn't care if they ever removed the handcuffs from Minnow. He looked forward to slapping them on the guy exactly the way the police did in the cop movies.

Their group signaled a right turn and exited the freeway. He thought this was the longest light he ever saw. The limousine was thankfully moving slowly north which was odd. Brake and his team were at the top of the off ramp waiting for the light to change when a Nevada motorcycle team approached alongside them. Brake knew the person was the second leader of the group.

The second leader smiled as if he knew a secret.

Next, he noticed the odd chrome job on the side of the motorcycle. The whole scene was off somehow. Brake scratched his head, because he knew he saw something critical. He snapped his fingers.

Brake looked again at the chrome, "Heavy artillery."

The Nevada group burst ahead of Brake's team, flying through the red light, and driving toward the limousine. Brake figured they missed the, No-Right-Turn-on-Red sign, which was a stupid thing to do unless a person wanted to pay a heavy fine. There always appeared some off-duty police person to write the ticket. It was usually the second person in the car, the one with the meter-maid mentality. Those women who checked the parked cars had eyes like an eagle or other super bird even on their day off. Brake looked around. He didn't see anyone that looked like those ladies.

A vehicle turned left, and Brake almost made the decision to run the light when two chrome painted machine guns were pulled off the motorcycles up ahead while the men were driving in the north side road. Two bikers fired a massive round of bullets into the back-passenger side of the limousine.

Brake knew there was no way Minnow survived the carnage. The limousine was a simple vehicle with no hidden armor. He decided the bullets were close enough. His team turned left on the green light and dispersed into groups of two. They removed themselves quickly from the area.

The Nevada team also disbursed.

Behind Brake's team was a rental car with two hit men from Miami hired by Domingo to take out Minnow. Seeing the fire power bend the limousine, they, too, turned left. They believed someone beat them to the job. The one man in the rider's seat disassembled their plastic guns and eventually threw the parts out the window on the way to the airport. It would take only minutes for the heavy trucks to crush the guns into polymer dust. Any leftover metal part would eventually roll into the ditch.

The Nevada group were one of the teams to break off from the large group when Randy took control of all Minnow's gangs. They kept all their illegal activities but were pissed the barn hadn't been replaced by Minnow. They had invested much of their time and money into the operation. It was only fifty thousand dollars, but it was their money which was gone. They knew Minnow accidentally forgot his debt to them.

Brake quickly contacted Randy who was surprised by the Nevada group's bold move. Randy let his leaders know to extricate their people from the 405 areas, because something heavy went down. Heavy meant massive police. He told them to stand clear of the

Nevada group. Stand clear meant to totally avoid the freaking area or be arrested.

XXXXXX

Derek flew by police helicopter to the scene which became a traffic nightmare for the police and ambulance to get through. The coroner was closer and heard the call.

Derek looked inside the limousine and watched the coroner.

"This man is dead."

"How many bullets?"

"I count at least ten. There might be more."

"Machine gun?"

"It probably is the type of weapon which hit him after he was already dead."

"Already dead? The man is dead from what?"

"The death appears to be anaphylactic shock. I'll be more solid after we do our tests."

"This is a new one. Bullets and shock. What type of allergen is involved?"

"Probably the crispy bar on the floor. The object smells familiar and probably contains some oil versus butter. It looks like the man's medicine bag in the back-seat pocket is empty. There is no medicine pen inside whatsoever. It is a strange thing, the nonexistence of the pen."

Derek interviewed the chauffeur who couldn't remember a thing. The ambulance tech thought the chauffeur developed a mini heart attack after turning off the ramp, which was probably caused by the gun the dead man carried and the later gunfire.

The police mentioned there were no witnesses who came forward. That type of behavior was expected. People wanted to get home and not be involved.

Calling Rhonda, Derek was informed that Randy was at his second restaurant reviewing the new security system. *He was there in the office.*

Derek was glad Randy wasn't directly involved. Consequently, Derek drove to the second restaurant and interrupted a meeting.

52   Meeting Interruption

RANDY'S PEOPLE STEPPED out to the bar. They would have to wait for information later. The police investigator took precedence over their meeting.

"Where were you two hours ago, and your gang members?"

"We were all here in my weekly meeting."

"Of course, you and your team were here. You look like you had a fight recently. Would you shed some light on the location and person who was involved in the fight?"

"Equipment failure at the gym; it happens all the time."

"A very dead Minnow also looks like he ran into equipment failure big time."

"Then, Minnow is really dead?"

Derek knew Randy didn't know about the actual cause of death. He sat down.

"Can I ask you for some whiskey? It's my favorite brand. I did notice the brand's bottle the last time I was here. Today, I have no resistance and will be heading home soon. My work is almost done."

A surprised Randy went to his expensive liquor cabinet and poured two drinks. He handed Derek his drink. Derek was holding some powerful information and was making Randy wait. Trying not to focus too much on the Los Angeles investigator, Randy sat down.

"I always am impressed with how they make the good stuff roll off a person's lips into the smoothest taste. It helps sometimes when the world is off. You probably know people who own machine guns."

"I'm glad you appreciate my smooth whiskey. Yes, I do know a few people that purchased some of those guns, but I don't know where those people moved recently. Some of them are in prison. The police should know about those people."

"Good answers."

Randy waited as he knew Derek would share the information shortly. Per Brake, the bullet firepower was extensive. From the distance, his gang were from the crime committed by the Nevada gang, the flare and spray of bullet fire at the scene was familiar to them.

"The bullets weren't what killed Minnow."

"Seriously?"

Now Randy was at a loss and he frowned. The odds that Minnow was not killed by bullets were so slim. Unless someone else took over a hit. Minnow's enemies grew in number lately, matching his schizophrenic and downward spiral. It was as if his brain were removing all positive feelings, letting madness own him. The synapses in the brain were obviously destroyed at an excessive level, leaving his aberrant thoughts to commit evil deeds. Evil deeds always tripped a person.

"Very seriously. He was already dead in the limousine before the bullets hit. The limousine was at a stop because the gas tank was registering empty. The chauffeur hadn't filled the tank."

"How can that kind of thing happen? I mean the bullets not being the cause."

"Was Minnow highly allergic to anything?"

"Yes, peanuts, but he always carried his medicine pen. Everyone has knowledge of this information because he was paranoid, and he constantly talked about his problem."

Derek made the decision to provide more information in the hope Randy would help the police solve the crime.

"The medicine case at the scene showed empty. He probably died from anaphylactic shock. The chauffeur can't remember a thing about driving the limousine or the man inside. He wasn't sure the passenger's name. He was surprised to see the bullet holes in his vehicle and the ambulance took him to the hospital for observation. There were no witnesses at the scene nor anyone contacting the police with information. We are awaiting the final coroner's report regarding Minnow Surf."

Randy sat there slowly drinking his whiskey thinking about Amy.

Derek knew he needed to wrap up this conversation, complete his report, and fly to the yacht. He didn't want to divulge too much information now. Besides, Randy was disappearing in front of him into memories of Amy.

"Do you want Minnow Surf's body for burial?"

"No, the gang already has voted."

Derek looked at Randy who let the information on a gang vote slip.

235

Randy shrugged. "Would you please place the dead body as far away from Amy's grave as possible?"

"I will strongly suggest Minnow's body be placed as far as possible. It is the best I can do for you."

Randy stood up and came around to Derek. He looked him in the eyes and shook his hand.

"Thank you."

Derek left the restaurant. He felt better already.

One of the evil con artists was dead. He knew in time, Randy would feel better. His gang probably didn't kill Minnow, but he thought Randy knew who did. He thought Randy knew who fired the round of bullets at the limousine, too. Derek wouldn't be surprised by the name of the person who removed the medicine pen. The Nevada group that tried to do the hit would be caught in the future.

53   The Cemetery

BRAKE WAITED UNTIL the workers covered Minnow's casket and left. He knew he was the only gang member that needed to make sure there was an end to the pollutant rat called Minnow. He came back to visit the grave a second time because he bought a pack of cigarettes at the small gas station store. The store was close by. He also bought a lighter rather than matches.

Looking around, he felt at ease. Cemeteries represented fond memories of beer parties and pretty girls. There were also the bottle throwing contests. Back then, they used aluminum cans which didn't go as far. Brake took a little gravel and put in his can. He won every time.

Sitting next to the grave, he took the pack and lighter out of his pocket. He looked up at a tree limb which looked like it was partially cracked. There were a bunch of dead leaves on the end. Brake pretended he held his gun, took fake aim, and shot the limb down for Amy.

He looked at the pack of cigarettes and slowly peeled a little wrapping off, then a little more, and suddenly there was a hole in the top of the pack. Caro wanted him to stop smoking. He tried for two weeks but was having some trouble today.

Brake looked at the branch again and wondered if he did his call-of-the-wild jungle yell, would the

237

noise cause the dead to rise? He would have to be on his motorcycle just in case. He didn't know if the dead carried weapons or not. It probably depended which gang they belonged.

Laying down on the grass he turned the pack and wiggled it a little bit. Nothing happened so he wiggled the pack a little more.

"A cigarette accidentally did fall out of my shirt pocket. Now, how did it do this trick?"

Brake put the rest of the pack down on the dirt over Minnow's grave and picked up the lighter flicking it closer and closer to the single cigarette.

"We have fire ladies and gentlemen. It is now okay to smoke the addictive limb."

Brake picked up the white object and smoked the cigarette. Checking his watch, the cemetery would close in ten minutes. He must leave. Brake already brought some white daisy seeds and water in his coffee cup that he spread at the head of Amy's grave. He said a prayer for her. He could only remember one now because his eyes were misting. He wore all black and looked respectful.

He stood up and flicked the cigarette butt toward Minnow's grave leaving the pack and lighter there. Brake decided it was time to ride away on his motorcycle. He rubbed a little dirt off the chrome before sitting on the bike's seat. The new bike seat felt good. Caro helped sew a leather extension.

Unfortunately, the cigarette lit the cigarette pack on fire. Whether it was the vibration of two semi-trucks hitting the pothole in the road on the nearby freeway or something else to create a cause and effect situation, failure would start happening.

Brake revved the engine, listening to the fine sound. He didn't hear anything because he put his helmet on. Tapping his horn a few times, he let go of the warbled jungle yell before taking off. He accidentally hit the open microphone on his music radio station which blared hard, electric guitar rock with pounding drums. Brake pounded the beat on his bike bars and revved the engine louder, squealing tires and yelling, "Yippee Ki-yay, you mother sucker."

The vibrations were too much. The branch cracked and fell on the small flame igniting the length of the grave and melting the lighter's cheap plastic case. The lighter fluid fueled a huge bonfire which lit the surrounding dry grass. The wind picked up a little more causing a spark of fire to light Brake's disappearing pirate bike flag, further adding to the disruption.

By the time the fire department arrived, there was a huge black spot surrounding a single grave. They quickly extinguished the fire. Witnesses told police there was a noisy, fiery blur that they saw on the cemetery road. Somehow, the image reminded them of a cemetery ghost movie they once saw called, Screaming Already Dead. The ghost in the movie wore black.

The next day, the cemetery workers returned to add more dirt because the water from the hoses sunk the ground on top of the grave. They returned several times to add more dirt to grave number thirteen hundred thirteen, Section D.

The workers knew it was a bad spot because the bush burned down and now all the highway trash floated into the sunken spot. They recognized gun metal parts and wondered how they arrived at this darn spot. They saw the orange-suited prison gang picking up the trash in the roadway ditches. The cemetery workers told themselves the plastic parts weren't real guns now that they were dismantled. The prison crew knew otherwise.

54   Afterwards

RANDY WORKED WITH his insurance company for a settlement amount on his bombed restaurant. The cleanup trucks hauled the burned bricks away from the restaurant. New dirt was added and graded. An architect was hired with a commercial builder, and plans approved. The building crew would begin immediately. A special food truck would be on the location as a temporary office for Randy.

Driving home, he picked up their luggage and suitcases, and placed them in his car. They were driving to the cruise ship pier in Los Angeles that would take them to Mexico. His boys would pick up the car from the parking lot as well as Brake and Caro's vehicle. Brake told Randy he needed a security team to protect him in case they ran into the bad bikers.

Brake brought special gear along for the trip just in case of trouble. He found some slightly used, two-person, survival life rafts that instantly blew up when the release was pulled. Storing them in a large duffel bag, he thought they would be safe if they needed to jump ship. Their room didn't have the extra storage, so Brake put them in Randy and Sandra's room.

Randy wasn't sure this trip would be a vacation or not. He would very much try to relax for Sandra's sake. She needed this trip to escape the madness in her world. Randy hoped the new restaurant would also cheer her up when it was completed. He let her pick her favorite red color for the interior.

Purchasing a new and much larger diamond ring set in expensive platinum for his wife with matching earrings made her happy. The old diamond flower ring was turned into a pawnshop and the money donated to charity.

Brake brought four cold opened beers to Randy's cruise cabin for a toast. Randy answered the door and groaned. Brake wore red shorts, a red flowered Hawaiian shirt, straw hat with red tennis shoes, and no socks. The huge neon red was too much for Sandra who turned away. She looked at Randy again and started laughing. She patted Brake on the shoulder and told him he was too much, but still fun. Brake was happy they approved. He knew Sandra liked the color red.

Randy went to his suitcase and brought out the second expensive pair of sunglasses he purchased.

"Here, Brake, you forgot something."

Brake put the new glasses on his head with the tag in the front.

"High tech stuff. Does it play music?"

"No."

"I know it doesn't."

Randy turned and looked at Brake.

"No cigarettes with lighter on this trip."

"Yes, sir."

"And Brake, one more thing."

"I do know the answer. No jungle yell when I jump off the high swim board. We don't want to be uncool."

Brake and Caro went to their cruise ship room and Caro looked sad. He knew the look.

"Baby, I see that you miss our Miss Aby doll kitty, but so do I. Our kitty is the only thing that gives me super kisses and rubs me like she does. We hired an intelligent capable person to take care of our kitty. You must relax so we can return as a happy people. I already purchased two new shaky toys for when we return."

"I know, and I will relax."

"Okay then, everything is good to go, because I have to concentrate on my job protecting our friends. I can't wipeout."

"You will do a good job like you always do."

Brake loved the way Caro looked now. He knew she was surprised when he took her to Las Vegas. It was the red dress and platform heels she wore while they gambled. He immediately proposed in their room in the evening and bought her a one carat diamond ring. He didn't want some guy to intervene and snatch her up. They married the next day in her white chiffon dress in one of the many local chapels.

It was exactly what Caro wanted to happen. Randy, Sandra, and the gang were pleased for them. They saw the friendship and love bloom between them. Randy knew it was Rhonda who helped Caro change her looks. He gave both women a raise. Caro became a permanent bartender at the nightclub taking classes at night to improve her bartending skills.

"You are the best cat wife."

Brake saw the price of his new sunglasses and almost fell out of his chair.

55   Amy's Letter

DEREK LOOKED AT his secretary who came into his office. It was a quiet time in the criminal world since Minnow passed away. He wondered about the fire surrounding the gravesite. It was almost as if the burnt ground was a reminder to the bad guys of their potential demise.

Another strange story was circulating of a race-type ghost traveling fast which scared people. The con artists thought it was another costume and mask worn by someone. Nobody knew anyone who owned a ghost costume. They were worried it was a gang of dragsters or foreigners in the area.

Opening the folder, there were the letters from Amy to Minnow while they were in jail, rubber banded with a note to read the back of the stamps for the location of the gun used to kill two gang leaders. There was a torn photo of his wife, Jess, with writing on the back. It read, "Easy Target."

Derek frowned. It bothered him.

"How did you know the words? You used Minnow's words and turned them against him for our first takedown project of the Nevada drug bust."

He drifted into thoughts regarding his wife. He remembered her face at their meeting in Puerto Vallarta. "You wanted the creep to lose it when he was dragged into court. You were going to show him that you were *no easy target.*"

Picking up the folder, he found what he wanted. He opened a letter typed on plain paper which looked like paper a lawyer used. But then it looked like any other company's office paper. Derek stared at the female's strange signature and then he read the note. Contemplating what to do with the letter, he asked his secretary to make a copy as he was leaving the office.

Randy was surprised to see Derek drive his sports car to the new restaurant site and park next to his vehicle in the other private space. His security people left Derek alone with Randy.

He pointed at the makeshift bar in the food truck and Derek nodded. Randy remembered their last conversation and drink. Something was off in the world.

Inside the food truck, Derek handed Randy the folder which contained only a copy of Amy's last known letter. He noted her signature which was the capital letter of her name drawn into a woman with flipped hair, then the eyes, nose, and lips. Next to the drawing were the last two letters. Randy couldn't help smiling. He read her letter and put it down.

Randy walked to the food truck door window and stared out. His expression was a blank.

Wondering if Randy saw anything at all out that window, Derek stood up.

"I thought the letter was important and wanted you to have a copy. I'll let myself out and I wish you luck on your new venture. I do mean it on a private level."

Derek left. Randy sat down and reread Amy's letter.

"If anyone is reading my letter, then Minnow did try to kill me. The destruction within him was always there. I should have been smarter. But in the end, I do realize I'm better. I did arrange the basket of peanut treats for the gang to eat. I wanted them to remember me fondly if something happened."

"Goodbye to the gang, especially you, Randy, the leader. You should continue providing others with layers of cover. I did feel protected whenever I was near you. You will select the correct path because your left brain is logical. Your conscious flies right. This ability will direct you to goodness. I will love the white daisies the group might place upon my grave."

Randy asked Brake to notify the leaders of a meeting. They could stop looking for Minnow's murderer. Amy took care of every gang member's problem.

He didn't know she was the person who killed Minnow.

56 Proposal

SKID MOVED THE bouquet of flowers to the table in his dining room of his home in San Diego. The candles were ready, the wine chilled, and his gourmet dinner in the warming oven. Rhonda was due home shortly. Maggie was staying with the Michaels for the evening. Skid checked the diamond ring in his pocket for the fifth time.

They lived with each other for six months and he knew it was time to propose. They loved each other, and he wanted to continue with a more secure relationship. He listed all his good points in his head in case she forgot.

Seeing her car in the driveway, he opened the wine and poured into the glasses. He lit the long stem candles. Rhonda stepped into the dining room and saw the setup. She smelled the casserole in the oven. She swallowed as Skid looked excited.

"Did I miss your birthday?"

"No, it is a special dinner. You need to relax. I'll bring the exotic casserole to the table with our salad and bread. I took off from work. I needed the time to make you bread."

She knew the bread making class was one of the one hundred classes he took.

Skid waited until they completed their dinner and ice cream dessert. He got down on his knees. He loved her, and she knew it.

"Please marry me so we can live forever in the enchanted forest of wonderful."

"Is there a ring in this strange and wonderful forest?"

Skid pulled the jeweler's box out, opened it, and placed the large, many-carat diamond ring on her finger. She told him some time ago her favorite metal was platinum.

Rhonda looked at the perfect ring and the love in his eyes.

"Let wonderful begin, and the sooner, the better. I've found the best place for a honeymoon. Can we do the honeymoon first?"

She didn't yet tell him she owned five times the money and assets that he did. She thought it would be a nice surprise on their honeymoon to the Grand Caymans. She hacked his computer and saw the websites and purchase of airline tickets. He knew she wanted to go there next on their places to visit.

Rhonda figured something was happening in their home. She wasn't a detective all these years without heavy skill sets in knowledge. Maggie would have another intelligent role model.

57   Final for Domingo

DEREK'S SECRETARY SAW the police report arrive in her mailbox. She read the report and texted Derek. He pulled over to the side of the road and read the information.

The head falcon no longer existed. Domingo's enemies were widely distributed. He entered the con artist game and became rich. To get rich, he conned many people and probably killed the same number.

Putting Domingo in jail started the closing of the nets for capture with no release. The other bad guys held their con game in for a long time allowing Domingo to feel safe. He could eat good food and occasionally have a stolen glass of wine. The library was extensively used along with the exercise equipment. He was in contact with his people all the time.

Nothing really changed too much in his life other than he missed a few parties. His tan looked great from spending time in the yard outside. The only thing wrong was his missing his two aging falcon birds.

His people arranged for a huge donation to a company in Los Angeles that took in rescued birds. Domingo was assured they would be well taken care of by this company who used them at an expensive hotel to scare away the pigeons. Domingo approved the deal and the secret money was withdrawn from a bank in Switzerland.

The scales of justice already tipped on Minnow Surf.

Domingo knew he was lucky to be rid of the scoundrel. What he didn't know was his time on this earth was hitting zero soon. The police death report picture showed an African Mamba snake skin.

Derek didn't need to read much further because he was familiar with the woman, the international hired assassin. Domingo met his demise in his cell and died from the extremely poisonous venom. The assumption was that the Snake woman was his killer.

The prison thought Domingo had no clue he was going to die because he paid one of the guards with money to buy cigarettes for delivery the next day. They weren't sure where the money came from that Domingo obtained. They found his mattress lined with wads of money. The prison checked the mattresses once a week.

Wondering how the woman managed this kill was impossible. The fancy, professionally laundered bed sheets were removed and thrown away making any trace of the poison difficult. The meal containing the fresh vegetables and fruit was placed in the garbage and the dishes sanitized. The cigarettes and money disappeared from the prison collection room.

The police tried to reach Domingo's lawyer and found his office in a high-rise building was empty. His secretary also disappeared. They found out from the office tenants across the hall, the woman left three weeks earlier. Unable to reach or find further information, they were at a standstill in the investigation.

The police put out a notice on the missing lawyer and the photo from the security camera at the stop light. The tenants mentioned the image was possibly the secretary. It was hard to tell with the large scarf and sunglasses the person wore.

The police really wanted to catch this illusive Snake person. They didn't even know her nationality or country of origin. The list of bodies in many countries were reaching a high number. The police began to believe there were more than one person involved. They believed someone met and worked with the Snake woman besides Domingo.

58   Shannen Initiates Search

MAX QUICKLY SLID the single report to Shannen across the table. He was out of breath. Reading the file, she looked up in alarm.

"No, I did not order the kill, nor would I ever do so. You know me."

Shannen looked out the window. They didn't initiate anything against Matin Domingo. She couldn't make the decision and it cost her dearly.

"Domingo's enemies are many. It is only a matter of time before someone would try to bring him down," said Max.

"Yes, I believe there are others. I didn't expect his death so soon and with my stolen poison and calling card. Matin would have known at the last moment that his imminent death was not performed by me. It is time for us to change our lives. Make the changes to remove all trace of my company's existence and tell the lawyer to sell the island. The planes and helicopters must be sold. The snakes must be donated to zoos or science."

Max worried about the stolen poison.

"The poison will need to be relocated. There are only a few samples of the old method. I checked the inventory and we are missing ten vials. The research will need to be destroyed. I suggest we burn the research building. Most of the research is stored on flash drives for me so I can separate the files. I'll pack those items in my small jewelry case. We will move to our second place and begin again. The place is unknown to my enemies and the police. Make sure the employees receive their final payments once you and I reach safety. Then you must close the account in a month."

"I will start the process immediately."

"What do you want me to do about the copycat killer?"

"Put the tracker on the project immediately and keep her on the payroll."

"Are you going to be all right? I don't want to leave you for even a moment."

"I will be fine. There is a time to be sad and this is not one of them. We must leave, because there is much for both of us to do before nightfall."

Shannen let the fires of revenge begin to start. Her tracker would find the person or group responsible. The movement was required because Domingo's lawyer disappeared, too. The police could be very close or someone else more dangerous could be close. They would leave to their second location immediately.

Max loaded her into the float plane with her standard suitcases as if she were taking a short vacation. She would fly to the designated small airport. He would follow in the incoming second float plane and meet her later.

He really didn't like their second place because it was cold most of the time. Max visited there only one time and it was many years in their past. He wondered how they would survive, because the town was some distance. The money was safe in hidden accounts and stored within the plane floats which would be removed at the private airport owned by an offshore company.

New passport and identification documents would show a change of name for both and a marriage certificate. Max was surprised by the last document wondering if the document changed their relationship.

He would be surprised at the massive difference done to the layout of her parent's estate. Living in the country in Russia would be an enjoyable time for the two of them. There would be plenty to do at their wilderness site. Their current operations would be off everyone's charts for a year while they pursued their search for the poison copycat.

Upon locating the copycat person, the set-up plan would be completed. The police would receive documents and a report to show them the path to catch the con artist. The lost Domingo lawyer would be among the criminals found in the foray.

The Snake woman, Shannen, was no one a con artist should try to out con. She was the master artist whose experience overrode theirs by a million miles. She always won in the game being the larger cat.

Domingo knew this piece of information. That was why he let her go when she decided to leave. She informed him, if she ever wanted to kill Domingo, she would look him in the eyes. Then she would kiss him goodbye, swiftly kill him, and silently walk away. She hadn't done those moves.

A decision by Shannen would need to be made after the poison assassins were captured. She knew how to kill them. That was not what worried her.

255

The dilemma would be for her and Max. The solution was either stay under cover, move to location three, or restart their operation. Events would happen to change all their future arrangements.

59   Catalina Island

DEREK WENT TO the pier and hopped aboard Jim's fifty-foot fishing tub. It was great fishing weather and would remain the same ninety-two-degree temperature all weekend. A breeze would pick up around noon. They went fishing early in the morning. It was lunch time and Jim would drop him off next to their yacht which was moored on Catalina Island. Derek retrieved the bouquet of flowers Jim placed below. The chef was waiting with the oysters and caviar. The champagne and strawberries were chilling. Justin and Sami were staying with the Michaels and were already with Mary Beth. The twin girls were on the yacht with their nurse caretaker.

Jess hugged her handsome husband after he stepped onboard, and she waved to Jim before taking her flowers. Her husband grabbed her and crushed some roses. He didn't care and kissed her a long time. Jim looked back to see the kiss.

"The boy is still tied up in knots over dream girl. Mary Beth, my wife, will not be surprised."

Derek went down to the lower level to visit their six-month-old daughters who tried to pull themselves into a wobbly step with their walkers. He picked them both up, hugged, and kissed them calling their names, Cata and Alina.

They jabbered their stories and he listened to them while Jess changed in their bedroom. He swung them around and told them his stories. Their eyes were sleepy when he sang them a lullaby. He carefully tucked them into bed with their bottles of milk. He called their nurse into the room and informed her that he and Jess were retiring for the evening. She already knew because the captain gave her the message.

Derek talked to the captain and gave the signal to their chef. Entering the master bedroom with the food cart and champagne, their chef left them alone. Derek opened the champagne and poured two glasses in the tall flutes. He opened the covered dishes and looked at Jess.

She knew he was hungry and skipped lunch.

"Please go ahead."

He took two bites of everything and held his flute to the other flute, connecting with her by touching her soft hand. He hit the remote to close all the shades and hit the button for soft lighting. He handed the remote to Jess because she wanted to select a song.

"To you, my sweet wife."

"Back at you, always."

Derek drank and put his glass down. He grabbed two more oysters. Taking her in his arms once more, he was reminded of the first time he saw her. It was the moment his world stopped, and the words hit him.

"I love, need, and want only you."

"A young knight once told me those words."

"Was the knight a very strong, handsome, and intelligent one?"

She knew the correct answer, or he would chase her around the room. "Yes, very handsome."

Derek looked at her. She remembered because her eyes sparkled at him. They were misty gray. Jess heard his love words before many times, but each time, they sounded new. She pushed her long blond hair off her shoulder.

Derek knew everything about Jess was complicated. If he entered her world, his life would change forever. He willingly did that very thing. He was swept away by her heart and his. He only wanted to breathe in her world. He was totally lost in her love and their possibilities.

That was a long time ago. He now felt confident in their love, having traversed major hurdles. But he never took her love for granted, always shielding her from everything bad. Every moment with his beautiful wife was precious to him. He looked at Jess and knew precious was about to happen.

Derek could wait for dinner. He started kissing his wife in all the spots he knew, matching the song's lifting desire. Jess chose the love song with the remote. There was a time to surrender to the roaring wind which was blowing passion into more love. The love arriving was more than what currently existed. The feelings mounted and matched his breath of air. Jess was his air and vice versa. The kaleidoscope color of their love matched the gorgeous flowing gown she wore.

He smelled peonies in her hair and Derek knew there was a little air left between them for another kaleidoscope. His wind was hers totally for the taking, her arms surrendering to him again, totally rocking his center of gravity. He gave to her everything. They found an enchanting private place for each other that no one could enter.

"For me, this is the *magical* about you," said Derek.

Derek knew there were three more females in his home that would break men's hearts. He was glad he found his one and only true heart. He left Jess sleeping and went back to the food cart. He made sure Jess ate enough earlier. Crawling into bed next to his wife, he heard a text message on his phone.

It was from Skid. "She said, yes."

Derek would tell Jess in the morning that she could help with a wedding in the future. He could see more designer dresses being drawn and the girls would help. Derek fell asleep with a smile on his face.

Jess crept out of bed and checked the text message on her cell phone. Rhonda said, "The dress is on."

Jess danced around the room. Rhonda wanted Jess to design her wedding dress. The two women looked at dresses on the computer. Some contemporary designs were drawn, and Jess sent them to her earlier in the week. Rhonda wanted amazing. Jess knew how to draw those concepts.

Jess could hardly wait to tell her husband in the morning. Romance was on the horizon for their two friends. She went back to bed and snuggled next to Derek who was sound asleep in a wonderful dream world. Life was going to be fun in their future. Jess also fell fast asleep on their secure yacht.

60   San Diego Wedding

THE WRIGHT'S ARMORED vehicle would take Jess, Derek, and the beautiful bride, Rhonda, to the large church. Jess was dressed in her pale blue sheer gown with massive rhinestone belt at the waist in a special design. The rhinestone colors separated to look like stripes from a skydiver parachute.

Rhonda's dress was a contemporary high-low style with folding layers of lace and tulle. The fabric was from Italy and the short front flowed down from the natural waistline. The gown was high in the front and long in the back, so she could dance better without tripping.

The top of the gown was strapless and looked like a folded tulip or a parachute canopy opening. While the long ten-foot train showed folded, rolling layers of fabric behind her, it detached later. Her belt contained the same rhinestone design in the softer silver colors. Her shoes were white lace ankle boot-high heels.

Her bouquet was massive quantities of white roses and lilies with green-leaved sprays. Skid bought Rhonda beautiful silver diamond dangle white pearl earrings from one of his favorite stores in Hong Kong. Simple white roses were in her tied back hair. Jess was glad she only carried three white lilies with navy satin ties to keep her hand free to smooth the flowing bridal gown train.

262

Waiting at the altar was Skid, Derek, and two of Skid's surfer male friends. The bridesmaids were Jess, Tami, and Ara. Maggie was the single flower girl. The dresses matched the same pale blue design. Sami wore a navy satin gown for her later performance. The men and Justin wore navy tuxedo jackets with pale blue satin lapels, bow ties, and matching navy pants.

It was time for Rhonda to walk down the aisle escorted by Jim Michaels. When Skid saw her, suddenly he couldn't breathe. Rhonda was walking too slowly down the aisle. He didn't wait and met his stunning bride halfway down the aisle. He glanced at her gorgeous dress and knew the bridal couture gown was perfection and fit her personality.

"Ready?"

"I'm so ready. Can we skip this part and arrive at our honeymoon early?"

"Never miss a party paid for by the Wrights. It's a major good time."

Skid tucked his arm within hers and walked with her the rest of the way. Holding her safe and secure so she didn't run away. Their vows were exchanged, and they were driven by a hired white limousine to the grand hotel in the ballroom on the twelfth floor which overlooked the Pacific Ocean for their reception party.

The cake was a large gourmet, five-foot, white fondant cake with white roses and blueberry filling. The caterers helped install a parachute over the cake with ties to keep the sky blue and white canopy open until the cake was completely cut and distributed. Additional white flower streamers hung from the ceiling adding to the surrounding array of flower bouquets.

The food was massive quantities of small meat or cheese sandwiches and puff pastry meat-filled canapes. Vegetarian canapes were on silver trays on the huge iced buffet table as well. There was a separate sushi bar close to the drink bar. A full bar kept the bartenders busy. The ballroom was opened to double its normal size to accommodate their extensive guest list.

The children's food table was mini vegetable or cheese pizza and batter-fried hot dogs. Various condiments were on the table in an airplane-designed silver tray. Fruit enveloped the cloud sculptured ice fountains which dripped champagne. There were tiny bottles of water and root beer for the younger crowd. Silver cardboard airplanes hung over the children's table.

Jess and Skid worked together to add a special guest to the reception. They switched bands and brought Wade Brookston's group in to play for the reception. Rhonda was fully surprised and delighted with the rocker performing her favorite songs. She wrote *Golden Girl* specifically for him, but he didn't release it until much later.

Wade danced midway in the song like the video, told his band to keep playing, and singled out the bride. He danced with her and talked.

"I'm here performing for you. It is my wedding gift plus I owe you big time for the *Golden Girl* song. How does five million dollars sound for your work?"

"What was your take on my song lyrics?"

"Probably thirty million or so. Maybe higher, because the song is continuing to outperform our expectations."

"I want seven and a half million and a decent percentage for the next five years of your net profits on the song. There is more. Plus, you will let your people know about Justin Wright. You will also help me when I ask you."

"Man, you're always all business. I wish you had stayed on my team. Can you please release to me and my lawyer your second song? I'm ready to roll with it."

Rhonda smiled. She knew he would give her whatever she asked.

"I'll talk with my lawyers about my second song, but we'll put it under my married name in the advertising."

"Let's twirl slowly and drive your real superman husband crazy. I'm agreeable to anything you need. Just call me. The second song is even more golden, like you."

Skid handed his champagne glass quickly to Derek knowing he needed to rescue his wife. He worried just a little when Wade danced too close to her on the stage, talked softly in her ear, and twirled her slowly in a secret love dance.

Approaching the two dancers, Rhonda whispered to Skid the amount of her take for the song lyrics on the first song. Skid enveloped Wade in a surprised hug and went back to Rhonda twirling her in his version of their love dance.

265

Wade would keep his promise to Rhonda and call Justin to perform their exact performance they did in Miami. The rocker knew it was all about the Rhonda connection to her beautiful friends. He was glad to be a part of the family. Rhonda told him the wonderful news that he belonged to something huge. Wade hadn't known family for a long time.

Rhonda insisted on inviting her other friends, Randy, Sandra, Brake, Caro, and two of the security teams at Randy's nightclub, believing a person needed all kinds of friends. Derek and Skid approved. Sandra and Caro were the ones who enjoyed a good time talking to high society women, admiring their designer gowns, and pricey jewelry. Their men seemed a little nervous being around so many police, high profile men, and obvious security. Randy developed a new respect for Derek and the people he knew in very top places.

The group saw the bride coming over to the gang table. Rhonda hugged each one of Randy's male team and conversed with the wives, further enhancing their friendship. They knew she married someone connectedly heavily with the police, but they knew her as a friend, good bartender, and excellent skydiving instructor.

She waved War Julio over to the table and introduced him to Randy who was pleased to meet the seafood tycoon who owned the large fishing business in Curacao. Randy knew what his chef's thought of the excellent fish he received from War Julio's businesses for his restaurants.

Her cover in the police operation was totally hidden from Randy's gang. All they saw was an easy-going person in love who was glad they came to her special day. They were impressed she knew the popular rocker who danced with her spellbound and treated her like a precious gift from heaven. They saw the new husband intervene. Everyone one saw the move.

They liked her friend, War Julio. He told them scary fishing stories and wrestling loose sharks on his boats. Then he told them a story about bad guy poachers and the use of plastic shark toys with real seals to catch them and hold them for the local police. He shared the name of the toy company with Brake and Randy. Brake would use some of the toys at their next party.

61 Honeymoon

RHONDA AND SKID'S honeymoon was located at the beautiful Grand Cayman Islands in the Caribbean because it was a British territory. Rhonda visited the area as a small child with her parents on their vacations.

The hotel was a posh five-star resort. They went snorkeling and diving for sunken ships. Skid told her the area was picked clean, but she didn't care. He painted some quarters with gold paint as a trick and left them on the ocean floor for her to find.

She caught on quickly and stuffed them in his new socks for their next dinner out on the catamaran cruise. Rhonda bought clothes at the ritzy shops while Skid read about the pirate festival in November. He told his new wife they should come back so he could wear one of his many costumes.

There was no end to their play during the day and evening. The two lovers fell deeper in lust. It was their special time and place. They would return and bring Maggie with them next time.

Arriving home, they looked at the wedding photographs and chose their selections. Their photographer took lots of pictures of them leaving the church and reception. Skid noticed two pictures of the roped off areas where the police held onlookers away from the wedding party and their dignitary guests. He pointed out the photos to Rhonda. It was the tracker woman with her high-powered camera.

They contacted Derek who received the photos. Derek called back Skid.

"I think that you need additional security. Do you want to call, or should I?"

"I'll take care of the additional people and invite the Cortez teams for an extended vacation to our home. Rhonda and Tami will be overjoyed at the visit. This is going to cost me with all the shopping my wife can manage in one day."

"That is a wise plan until we have more information. I'm sure they will invite Jess shopping. Then I will pay the price. Be safe."

"We'll do that very thing."

Derek pondered and worried about the game headed their way. Something was off, and Jess agreed with him.

"The con artists are constantly on the move. The scales are tipping again. I feel edgy."

"I also have the same feelings. There is limited information regarding the tracker. Limited means the large part of the iceberg is hidden. We'll have to bring out the heavy ammo like bombs or the bazooka. Rhonda knows how to fire both off. Perhaps the tracker woman doesn't know those facts. In any police case, the game constantly evolves into more risk. We've been fortunate not to have gotten injured."

Derek held his sweet wife, Jess, a little closer.

62   A Miami Woman Found

THE MIAMI POLICE contacted Derek about a strange death. The woman owned expensive camera equipment. The police reviewed the camera chip and were surprised to see wedding shots with Derek and his family in the pictures. They wondered if Derek knew the woman, because all identification was removed from her apartment. The detective had worked with Rhonda in the past and was happy to view some of her wedding shots.

Derek flew to Miami and met his well-known detective friends.

The woman was registered as Coral Hanson with the apartment application. There was a roommate that the neighbors thought was a man, but they weren't sure. The roommate was missing, and the police were looking for the person. The woman was listed as a self-employed consultant with Hanson's Investigations.

The death was a strange one as was the tattoo around her neck.

They showed Derek the coroner's report and the dead woman's photos. The woman was the person tracking Rhonda and Skid. She was the person who followed them to the Grand Cayman Islands. Derek explained the woman tracker's movements over the last several months and the limited information he had acquired. He looked again at the tattoo which looked like a rope with a snake head.

He read again the coroner's report.

"She suffocated on a key, keyring, and plastic fob. What is the key? It looks similar to a bank deposit box key? Did the police check with the banks? Do they think the death is a suicide?"

"We aren't sure about the death, except for the key. The key is a bank box. Inside the box are lists of transactions between the woman and her clients."

The detective handed Derek another set of papers which contained dollar amounts, dates, name with address and phone numbers. The paper showed deposits for consultation work with clients.

Derek read the names and stopped at one name. He couldn't believe what he saw. The detective friend nodded. Derek told the detective that he would handle the interview with the person and provide the detective with his report.

"Our person may be able to provide information if she met the roommate."

The detective was relieved to pass the interview off to Derek. "There is one more thing. The woman owned a supped-up red sports car with expensive silver rimmed wheel covers and we can't find any record of her purchasing the vehicle. On the list is a man's name in Los Angeles with a circle around it. But there are other names with circles. The vehicle contains a sticker about Los Angeles. The police will see if there is any significance to the annotation and the VIN number of the sports car."

"Is there a photograph of the red sports car?"

"Sure, there are two photos in my briefcase."

Looking at the photographs, Derek told the detective, "Check the vehicle identification number against the list of sold vehicles from the last Los Angeles police auction. I'm certain there exists a match because the driver door looks repainted. There was a sports car with a door removed at a chop-shop incident a while back that involved Minnow Surf. The car looks similar."

The detective frowned and then brightened.

"Tell Rhonda we loved seeing her happy face in the photos. The view of her dress was great."

Derek called Rhonda to meet him at his special warehouse in Los Angeles after he arrived. He needed to talk with her privately about the tracker woman. He let her know the woman was dead in Miami.

63   Rhonda's Old Boyfriend

RHONDA KNOCKED ON the warehouse door and Derek opened it. "Hello, it's nice seeing you again. Let's go into the library and sit in comfortable chairs."

Grabbing two cold bottles of water, Derek handed her one.

"You don't need to sweet talk me, but it is nice to see you again. I feel rested from my honeymoon and am adjusting to married life."

"Good. I talked with your husband, Skid, before I flew to Miami and he was still bouncing off the walls."

Rhonda smiled. "Do you think Skid could live in a high-rise building with a helicopter pad? I'm researching properties and am thinking about owning a building. Wade's lawyer has approved my second song lyric deal so there will be money arriving at my bank in a couple weeks. I also don't know what type of helicopter to purchase for my husband's birthday. Do you have any suggestions?"

"Congratulations on the song deal. As far as the rest, wow, you are too much."

"Yeah, I used to get the same reaction from my dates."

"Your husband might want to choose his own helicopter and select the options. He knows lots of technical pieces on each brand. We have talked many times about flying them. You can go together to the

273

manufacturer. Also, you'll need to ask him about the building because he may want two heli-pads.

Rhonda couldn't help it. She laughed. The second pad would be for the Wright's machine.

"Your wife told me about the two companies willing to purchase her bridal designs."

"Yes, she wants to see how well the designs do in the market before starting her own company."

"Her designs are beautiful and very in style. The market will love the designs."

Then she looked at Derek who was ready to tell her the Miami incident. She knew he also wanted to go home to Jess.

"Talking in private is important in case there are very personal issues you don't want revealed."

"I appreciate the private meeting."

Explaining to Rhonda the information he received from the Miami police and the strange death, he showed her a copy of the deposit pages. She saw her name and the amount of twenty-five thousand dollars. It was the amount she paid for an investigator to track her superman boyfriend.

"I was in my insecure phase worrying about the activities of my boyfriend. I did feel that something was very wrong. My boyfriend was gone frequently on trips, but so was I. It is a feeling about our relationship which seemed out of place due to his distracted nature upon returning home. I did see an ad in a Miami newspaper for investigative services. Having met with a man, I did sign a contract for their services, and gave them my check. The person I met seems like a man, but

I wasn't sure. They followed my boyfriend, took photographs of him with four other women, and handed me an extensive report, including a background check."

"Do you have the document and canceled check?"

"Yes, my accountant keeps my files."

Derek handed her a release form which she signed to allow him access to the information. The information would be handed over to the Miami detective.

"Can you meet with a police sketch artist soon, so we can provide a bulletin to the police about the possible photo of the roommate?"

"Yes, I will do so."

Derek showed her the photo of the dead woman with the even stranger tattoo. Rhonda shook her head, because she never saw anything like it.

"The tattoo is a custom job, successfully executed. Whoever does the ink most definitely will not share the client's real name because there may be more than one person in the group who wears the design."

"Interesting speculation. I'll let the detective in Miami know. The detectives liked seeing your happy face in the wedding photographs."

Rhonda laughed. She remembered one of the wedding photographs. "Yes, they do like to watch my legs."

"I recommend you inform Skid of our meeting, but probably not the detective's heated comments."

"Yes, my husband knows some of the stories about the unfaithful boyfriend, but not the part about a hired investigator. He does know my stories about the Miami detectives."

"I'm sorry you must involve Skid; but from a man's perspective, a husband will understand, especially if he can handle your Miami boys."

Rhonda nodded.

"Are you going to release the Safe House person?"

"Yes, the repercussions from Domingo or the Nevada gang are over. Those Nevada members should be in prison for some time. Plus, her recovery is coming along fine."

"The timing of your arrival in Los Angeles that day and the quick response from the police helicopter were amazing. The young woman should be thankful. By the way, your plan did work brilliantly."

"Yes, the woman is thankful and can now have a life of her own. The plan was perfect."

It was time for Rhonda to leave. She left Derek alone.

He would have to involve Jess in the new Miami incident. There could be so much more to the circumstances of the tracker woman's death. Derek wrote down the name of the old boyfriend. He had been totally surprised when Rhonda told him the name. The name was a familiar one in Miami. The person was part of the very rich, elite families. The ability to get any information from the man would be limited by the family's string of company lawyers. It would be a delicate line for the Miami police to walk. The Wrights knew the Miami family and invited them to some of their annual parties held there. Derek was glad he would be out of the game in solving this bizarre death case.

64   Release from Safe House

DEREK LOOKED AT the young woman beside him. She wore a new black dress with crème trim and crème tennis shoes. She looked calm and happy. The young woman helped the police and remained hidden in a safe house per their agreement. They allowed her new boyfriend to visit her on weekends only if he agreed to remain silent. The timeframe took nine months from the fake funeral.

The police found that sixteen out of twenty crispy treats contained peanut butter and were clearly labeled on the bottom. Four of the crispy bars contained plain marshmallow and were labeled as such on the bottom. A new baker who was filling in for the owner inadvertently made the mistake of putting the white icing on all the crispy bars instead of just the plain ones. The peanut butter bars should have had the maple frosting instead. When Amy gave the order to her friend, Caro, the delivery was to be dropped at the house she and Minnow lived. The basket was a gift for the gang in case of her untimely death.

Knowing Minnow used his last medicine pen in Encinitas outside the pawnshop, the police knew he never renewed or ordered additional medicine. Amy was the one who usually brought home his medicine from the pharmacy in the past and reminded Minnow of his doctor appointments. There was a chalkboard in the kitchen in her handwriting as a reminder to stop at the pharmacy.

They believed in his heightened frenzy to reach Miami and the number of drugs in his system were what caused him to eat the crispy bars. The police viewed the recorded rocker concert in Miami on the elderly chauffeur's television with clear view of the Wright family. Minnow previously had hit the record button.

The basket with the remaining crispy treats were on the kitchen counter with the uncleaned food plates in the sink, empty beer bottles, and garbage overflowing onto the floor.

There was a partial box of bullets which matched the revolver in the back seat of the limousine. The revolver and bullets showed a ballistic test match to the bullet removed from Amy Surf's side.

Derek had driven to Amy's beauty shop to talk with her that fateful day about turning against Minnow. Finding her shot and bleeding at the back of the shop, he knew she needed immediate help. He quickly took photos of the scene after contacting the hospital to be prepared for a gunshot victim.

Pressing his shirt on the wound to stop the flow of blood, Derek contacted the police helicopter which was near his location per the last radio transmission. He called the police helicopter which landed in the road, and they whisked her away to the closest hospital heli-pad. The doctors removed the bullet and cleared the shattered bones from the area.

They convinced her office manager to play along with the fake death and go on a round-the-world cruise. The boyfriend was brought into the fake story as well as the coroner and funeral home.

Randy hadn't wanted to view her body. Her boyfriend made the identification with the coroner.

Amy was whisked away to a safe house to heal, recover, and await out the drama. The whole plan was to catch Minnow and anyone who was connected to his illegal activities.

Derek was pleased with the results of the long investigation and turn of events.

"Are you sure that you're ready?"

She nodded. Amy looked in the rear-view mirror which caused Derek to do the same. In the rear-view mirror was Amy's boyfriend in his expensive sports car who would take Amy home to his new luxury apartment in Los Angeles. But first, she needed to explain everything to Randy. She didn't need him to protect her anymore. But she wanted to thank him.

Amy walked with her cane through the door of Randy's nightclub office because the security guard recognized her immediately. In this business, the security people were never surprised about anything. Randy looked up and quickly came to help her.

"It can't really be your wonderful body walking in my office? *How can you be alive?*"

"It's because of Derek Wright who did find and save me that day. Minnow shot me with his gun. I should have thrown that gun away a long time ago. It was bad luck. Or Minnow with it in his hands was the bad luck."

Randy remembered the gun. He should have taken it away from her.

"Minnow left me to die. He wasn't even sorry."

"I'm sorry Minnow hurt you. But your friend, Derek, used the gang and me to hunt for Minnow. They conned me in the game. Yet, I'm pleased with the result. You're alive."

"Yes, I'm the one who helped the police as well. It was time for me to take control and stand up for myself."

"You didn't kill Minnow. I thought you did but was unsure."

"No, I didn't kill him. His laziness, haste, or lack of money made him forget to refill his lifesaving prescription. He didn't read the label on the bottom of the crispy bars which were clearly marked. He assumed the bars were all the same. He must have been in a heightened, confused state of madness. I did see the madness when he shot me. I'm glad that he is gone and out of my life."

Randy tenderly hugged her and led her to one of his comfortable chairs.

"Thank you, for being my good friend. Tell everyone I'm fine. I love them for their loyalty. Remaining hidden until the police operation was over stopped Minnow from finding me. We waited until the ramifications of Matin Domingo's imprisonment plus the Nevada gang were lessened. That one gang would blame me for the loss of the Nevada Drug operation and their capture."

Randy gave her time to catch her breath.

"My hidden time in a Safe House was not wasted, because I took college classes online. I'm going to live my dream and get all the right credentials. I want to be somebody. I found a person who is good to me. We'll take care of each other. My doctor told me that I can throw the cane away in another month, but it will be a little longer before I can wear my heels. I must leave as my realtor boyfriend is waiting. I will send you the new address and phone number, so we can talk."

"You are somebody. You don't need to prove yourself to me or the gang. We love you, too. We are glad you're alive. Will you come back on occasion for a visit?"

She stood up and Randy moved to her side. She kissed Randy.

"Always. You must tell Sandra that we'll do lunch soon."

Randy walked her to the door. He kissed her once more and held her tight.

"One more thing. I took my ten thousand dollars and asked the lawyer to set up a beauty shop business called Amy's More Beautiful Shoppe and list Minnow Surf as one of my partners. Then I took a million-dollar life insurance policy on my business partner because of his value to my company. They are mailing me a check for the full amount."

Randy couldn't help but grin. "You are smarter."

He gave a salute to Derek.

Amy and her friend waved as they left in the sports car.

Randy called a short meeting with his gang. They would arrange a surprise party for her in the future when she could wear her heels. Amy would want to look exceptionally beautiful. Sandra would help in the beauty department showing her the best shops. Caro could show her their new collection of restaurant napkins and the pencils in the glass. The napkins showed the words: Write on me.

Derek smiled and drove home to his yacht family. Jess would be pleased with the outcome. It was a very wonderful day for Amy and Randy. They were in good company.

65   Race Car Driver

WHAT DEREK DIDN'T know was a new crime was being committed in Los Angeles. A race car driver finished his tall latte coffee and went back to his crew on the track. The crew was concerned about the right front tire not holding enough air. The race car driver would take his white supreme boss car around one lap and return to the pit area. The horsepower, torque and acceleration pulled the race car to top technical performance with the new air. Three-fourths of the way around the track, the vehicle slowed speed, and hit the padded side barrier stopping on the track. His crew raced to him and contacted an ambulance visiting the track that day. The ambulance took him immediately to the hospital.

The doctor knew Derek Wright from previous poison cases and checked for a specific poison. Then the doctor remembered their conversation about Snake woman. It was the Mamba snake poison that the driver had in his system. The dose wasn't strong because he only took a sip of the drink. The race car driver was given the antidote and was lucky to be alive.

The police would be involved in solving another poison case. There was nothing simple to attempted murder. Derek would need to untangle the mess to find a connection.

Pulling Rhonda with Derek to interview the well-known race car driver, they drove to the hospital to talk with the man. Entering the room, they were surprised to see a healthy young man with large bouquets of flowers, several women, and race buddies along with his lawyer. Derek and Rhonda introduced themselves and the guests left the hospital room, except for his lawyer.

"Mr. Palla, we are here to talk with you about your recent activities leading up to the time you passed out unconscious on the race track from a low dosage of Mamba snake poison."

"Call me, Mic. That's what my friends call me and the media. My real name is Henri which I detest. It is way too tame a name for my livelihood. My friends adopted the name, Mic, for me, because I always grab the microphone out of the news person's hands, especially the pretty female ones. You know I have to get the babe's attention."

Rhonda raised her eyebrows when Derek looked over at her. He thought this conversation would be interesting and swingy or maybe the word was racy. The man drove in circles for a living or perhaps it was ovals. It had been a long time since Derek went to a race track. He would need help there. Jim Michaels liked the race teams.

"By the way, I very much like glamour girl standing next to you. Are you free this evening? I can order something delicious brought into my unglamorous room, but we can turn the lights off and sneak some candles in the room. I did see some pink candles at the nurse's station. Do you have any matches?"

Derek looked at Rhonda. Rhonda signaled to Derek that she would take the next conversation because she knew all about local boys. This one was a known type to most woman.

"Perhaps you don't understand how dangerous this particular exotic African poison is to your system. It was given to you by a hired master assassin? The words are life and death situation which means no more babes and the end to racing on these local boy tracks. Heaven might have race cars. Perhaps you will let us know next time."

Derek stood there stunned. Mic was used to strife with women and was on instant replay.

"Ouch, you are tough, but impressive. Glamour, I step between life and death in a throw down dance every time I position myself in my race car and hurl down the track. Anything could pop on my car. That doesn't count the tags or bumps on my car from the other favorite and sometimes unfriendly competitive drivers' cars. The adrenalin rush alone is enough to give a person a heart attack. Each day is a miracle that I'm still standing. Prayer works every time. Heaven does have their own version of local race cars for us pretty boys. Red ones aren't allowed. They're too much of a good time because the boys like to crash those cars. That's why I drive any other color. Red is for off track when I'm driving your speed. You didn't answer my other question."

Rhonda smiled remembering the adrenalin rush from her last jump. This Mic person was funny and interesting. She read the dossier on Mic Palla regarding the number of race wins and position standings which were impressive statistics. There were the man's five divorces in less than ten years which showed a fast, action-packed time. She could see the attraction factor and the red car.

She showed him her huge new wedding ring. "The answers are no dinner and no matches."

"I'm clearly upset. My dinner this evening will be depressing. Whenever you want to replace that metal, you should give me a call."

Derek needed to rescue her, because he could tell she was ready to remove her gun. "Do you have anyone who wants to cause you harm?"

"As far as your questions, all I remember is driving, feeling a tingling sensation, which caused me to step on the brake, and then I can't move anything. I thought someone slipped me a mind-altering drug in my coffee latte that I purchased at the track food court. I was seeing a hula girl swinging on the tiny dash which I know shouldn't be there. The girl was plastic. Or my other thought scrambled in my mind before blacking out, some other race car driver wanted me to flat-line. In normal people's understanding, the word is retired."

Rhonda shook her head, "Did you really see a plastic hula girl?"

Mic grinned. "I got you, didn't I?"

Mic signaled his lawyer who produced four typewritten pages of names, addresses, and phone numbers. Derek hadn't expected the list so soon.

Mic noticed the surprise. "I thought everyone kept a list of enemies. I even categorize mine into groups from sort-of-savory to extremely unsavory."

Derek read the names.

"My ex-wives are on the list. We don't see each other too much anymore. They are in the middle group. Their manipulations of the truth are always suspect. They only contact me when they want something expensive. However, they will be delighted someone did try to wipe me out."

The nurse entered his room with the doctor who shook Derek's hand.

"Rhonda and I will check out the list of names. We recommend that you hire extra security and stay safe. If you remember anything, you need to call me."

Derek handed Mic and his lawyer his business card.

Mic leaned out of his bed, so Rhonda could see him. "Goodbye, Glamour. I like your stilettos."

Stepping outside the hospital room, the news media tried to break through the police. Derek and Rhonda were ushered into the doctor's office who would meet with them shortly.

"Don't even say a thing."

Derek appeared bemused. He wasn't going to touch the subject. He saw the man, Mic, breathless with infatuation about women, stilettos, and the whole package. The man also bordered on the driving edge of

288

miracles with cars and women. Derek felt old and very married. He was glad. He turned to Rhonda on their return flight, "You do know the expression. For men, with age, comes wisdom."

Rhonda couldn't help but laugh. It took Derek a day to explain to her something she already knew.

66   Assassin Profile and Hurdles

DRIVING BACK TO Derek's office, they pulled up the Snake woman's recent profile completed by the police psychologist. They both knew the lengthy report of kills completed and their locations. No known pictures existed of her which might have helped. The woman must be older now. What they didn't know was her age and when she began her killing spree?

"There is something wrong with the woman's profile and the attempted murder of the race car driver, Mic Palla."

"I'm feeling it, too. Something is not right."

Derek ran his hands through his hair. "Where is the link? Does there need to be a link? Heck, I have no idea."

"That is the answer. The poison used is an older version poison like her first hits, a slower acting one, which the Snake woman has not used in several years. There is the wrong link. The dose is too low, meaning the person didn't know its strength or did they realize it? The real assassin, the international poison woman knows exactly how much to administer for the kill. In either case, it was good that Mic didn't drink his coffee entirely."

"You're right. Her recent poisons are more sophisticated and swift."

Rhonda looked at Derek. "We need to focus on the wrong linkage. Of course, the other answer is the lack of swiftness. This attempt was made to create confusion and fear. It might have been a trial run."

"The Snake woman doesn't operate that way. She kills immediately and coldly. This is the second bad chink in a hit that doesn't fit her profile," commented Derek.

"So, we have a similar assassin, not as highly-educated or as worldly. Are they hired hits or is some other psychopath on the loose? The person could be an inexperienced copycat who plays with the victim in a cat and mouse game."

Derek nodded agreement. "It is definitely a smaller cat selecting spotlighted celebrities."

"You don't think the list will divulge someone close to Mic as the assassin?"

"I don't want to rule anything out just yet. There are other connections in the racing world we need to explore which are the extensive list of supporting companies and their teams."

Derek knew things in this investigation were a huge amount of work. He continued the conversation with Rhonda.

"The real Snake woman might appear if she is aware of the copycat. I believe she is an expert on knowledge at our level and the con artist sphere. She lives in their world as the master. She will want the person removed more than the police. She may create her own cat and mouse game to catch an imposter."

Rhonda's assessment had been similar, but she hadn't counted on the woman's own cat and mouse game. It was so simple. This woman was bright, acknowledged Rhonda.

Derek said, "We must complete the research on the list of names the lawyer gave us. We must jack up our game because the next big race day is only two and a half months away. Mic should agree to the police plan, the Race Commission would have to be contacted, and the spectators in the stands need to watch their show. There would need to be a plan of protection, emergency personnel, fake setups, and huge pieces of cheese for the capture plan."

Rhonda chuckled. She knew he threw the cheese into the scenario to distract her because it was getting close to the end of the day.

Leaving him to contact his superiors, she informed him, "I will start with the list regarding the wives. A person loves to hear delicious stories regarding ex-husbands."

"Thanks, Rhonda, I'm glad you did decide to stay onboard for this one."

"I wouldn't miss it for the world. I can watch glamour boy flaunt his Casanova stuff. That show alone is worth the high price of admission and that doesn't count the racing part of the equation. Besides, Skid enjoys placing bets on a winner at the speedway. I hear the speedway stadium is expanded and we both will enjoy researching the place together."

"Great, and for now, I'm glad to be in Los Angeles. See you later."

Derek rushed to catch his driver who arrived to pick him up at the airport. He glanced at the white Hollywood sign which he thought they should paint with a little glitter paint next time. His yacht was moored off Catalina Island. The helicopter was waiting for him at his warehouse.

He was ready to roll. He picked up his phone to talk with his wife. She was the swingy company he wanted this evening. She was his only major babe. He smiled when he heard her calm voice. Her conversation was one of those special times.

"It's me honey. I'm on my way home."

Derek understood the man named Mic Palla. He felt lucky. His group and the police would try to protect the race car driver. They would pull all their resources into the fray. Every little thing would be analyzed. Jess would be brought into the plan. Derek felt confident.

His cell phone rang.

Tami told him about her sister, Tiare Cortez, who just graduated from the Police Academy. Her sister had once dated a race car driver in the past who was still on the circuit. Derek remembered her as a pretty girl at their annual parties. Both women were free in their current schedules to help with Derek's upcoming investigation.

Derek smiled. Sometimes good things just walked up the street. This would improve the odds in their favor. Jess would be pleased.

"Oh, yeah, it will be a magnificent night." Derek began singing a favorite opera song.

Unknown to everyone, more than one evil game started, and the drama was on a fast roll with marked dice. The question would arise: Who and what was winning the race? Win was the only option currently open for grabs. Guess who began congregating? Revelation was around the next track.

More Exciting Books
in A Wright Series
by Author

Linda McKown